"Why don't you go sit with her?"

He swallowed at the Spirit's prompting. That was the last thing he wanted to do. First, he didn't want her to think he was interested. Second, she may have a date coming. Third, it would embarrass him to just walk up to her and say *you look a little lonely. May I join you?* And fourth...he couldn't think of a fourth.

Just ask her.

Swallowing hard, heat rose up his cheeks as he made his way to the front of the restaurant. He could just turn around, ask the cashier to bag it up, and go home. The idea was tempting, but the nudging of the Spirit was stronger.

He made it to the edge of the table. She looked up, a scowl wrapping her features. *So much for a warm welcome.* He forced himself to smile as he nodded across from her. "Mind if I join you?"

JENNIFER JOHNSON

and the world's most supportive redhead have been happily married for over two decades. They have three of the most beautiful daughters on the planet and one amazing son-in-law. Jennifer is a sixth-grade Writing teacher in Lawrenceburg, Kentucky. She is also a member of American Christian Fiction Writers. When she isn't teaching or writing, she enjoys shopping with her daughters, hanging out with her husband, Al, or her best friend, Robin, and playing on Facebook. Blessed beyond measure by her heavenly Father, Jennifer hopes to always think like a child—bigger than she can imagine and with complete faith. She'd love to hear from you. Email her at jenwrites4god@bellsouth.net or visit her website, www.jenniferjohnsonbooks.com.

Books by Jennifer Johnson

HEARTSONG PRESENTS

HP725—*By His Hand*
HP738—*Picket Fence Pursuit*
HP766—*Pursuing the Goal*
HP802—*In Pursuit of Peace*
HP866—*Finding Home*
HP882—*For Better or Worse*

HP901—*Gaining Love*
HP920—*Maid to Love*
HP938—*Betting on Love*
HP954—*Game of Love*
HP985—*Shoebox Surprise*
HP1013—*Pantry Promises*

Baby
Blessings

Jennifer Johnson

Heartsong Presents

To my Barbour Publishing family—
I love you all, but allow me to mention a few specifically.

I will be forever thankful to Jim and Tracie Peterson, who were willing to give
my writing a try. Aaron McCarver has been one of my greatest encouragers,
and he was a terrific editor. Laura Young and I have emailed enough that
she could be called my cyber BFF. How I appreciate your hard work.
And JoAnne Simmons! When the new editor came along, I feared what
the relationship would be like, but JoAnne Simmons was and is one of the
sweetest, most godly women I know. I have absolutely loved the last seven years
of writing Heartsong Presents stories. Barbour family, you have been such an
inspiration and encouragement to me. I have enjoyed working with you!

A note from the Author:

*I love to hear from my readers! You may correspond with me
by writing:*

Jennifer Johnson
Author Relations
P.O. Box 9048
Buffalo, NY 14240-9048

ISBN-13: 978-0-373-48640-3

BABY BLESSINGS

This edition issued by special arrangement with Barbour Publishing,
Inc., 1810 Barbour Drive, Uhrichsville, Ohio, U.S.A.

Chapter 1

Sabrina burst through her sister's apartment door. She bit back the urge to reprimand the college freshman for leaving the entrance unlocked. Again. She needed to find her sister. The text said it was urgent. Scanning the small living area, she spied only empty paper plates and cups on end tables. Mismatched shoes and various textbooks on the floor. "Mallory, where are you? What did you need to tell me that couldn't wait till morning?"

Pulling off the light brown jacket that did little to ward off Greenfield, Tennessee's cool, mid-October temperature, she tossed it on the couch. She wanted to slip out of her heels. It had been almost eight o'clock before she'd been able to leave the coffee shop then she'd headed to the gym for a quick workout then the store, where she'd received the disconcerting text message from Mallory.

She looked at her watch. Where were her sister's roommates? It seemed odd they wouldn't be home at well past eleven on a Thursday night. She sighed when she remembered the nickname for the evening when she'd been in college. Thirsty Thursday—club night. Most likely the girls wouldn't be home for several hours.

The faint sound of sniffles drifted from the hallway. Sabrina furrowed her brow. Her sister was known for embellishing stories, making things bigger than they really were. But she rarely cried.

Sabrina's heartbeat sped up. Surely nothing bad had happened. She squeezed her eyes shut as she thought of the many close calls she'd had in college. Times she'd drunk too much and found herself in situations that could have landed her in harm's way or jail. One particular time raced through her mind, and she sucked in a breath and swallowed. *Don't go there. No need to think about that.*

She pushed forward toward the soft cries. "Mallory?"

"I'm in here."

Her sister's voice trembled, and Sabrina bit her bottom lip. *Stop freaking out. It's probably nothing. Most likely, it's something silly. Maybe the girls didn't invite her to go with them.*

A smile spread her lips, and she bit back a chuckle. That was probably it. Nothing as bad as Sabrina feared. But then, Mallory had complained on several occasions that her roommates' lifestyle didn't mesh with hers and that she'd decided to find new ones for the next semester. Sabrina huffed. She liked the other girls. They'd all gotten along just fine until Mallory decided to go all churchy on them.

Shoving the thoughts away, Sabrina lifted her shoulders and pushed open the bathroom door. Her sister, eleven years her junior, sat on the top of the toilet seat. Her long dark tresses flowed past both slumped shoulders. Red splotches surrounded deep brown eyes. Most of their family and friends felt she and Mallory favored one another, which suited Sabrina just fine since Mallory had won more beauty pageants than she had fingers to count them. But then Sabrina had won a few herself more than a decade ago.

She moved to the tub and sat down on the edge. Wrapping her arm around Mallory's shoulder, she cooed, "Honey, what is it?" With her free hand, she pulled some toilet paper off the roll and dabbed at her sister's cheeks. "It can't be as bad as all this."

Mallory sucked in a trembling breath. She didn't say anything, simply pointed to the sink. Sabrina's heart skipped when she saw the white stick. *Oh no. Please no!*

Closing her eyes, she released her sister and forced herself to stand. She swallowed the knot in her throat. This couldn't be happening. Not to Mallory. She was too young. She had too much potential.

Sabrina opened her eyes. Two bright pink lines stared up at her. She shook her head and looked back at Mallory. "Maybe it's wrong. It happens all the time."

Mallory crossed her arms in front of her chest. "I'm late."

"How late?"

"Four weeks."

Sabrina stared down at her sister. "How can that be? Surely, you'd notice if you missed a whole period."

Mallory's chest heaved and tears streamed down her cheeks. "I did notice. I just couldn't believe it was possible. It was just one night."

Just one night. The three words wrapped around Sabrina until she felt she would choke. Reminding herself to continue to breathe, she pressed her hand against the doorjamb and leaned against the sink. "What are you going to do?"

Mallory hopped off the commode seat and jerked her

hand through the air. "Looks like I'm going to have a baby."

Sabrina swallowed again as she wrapped her fingers around the edge of the sink. More than a decade ago she would have suggested her sister consider abortion. Her stomach churned, and bile rose in the back of her throat. But now she wouldn't. Couldn't.

Sabrina's mind raced with what needed to happen now. How they would handle this. She cringed when she thought of their parents. She knew how they would react. "Well, you'll need to tell Randy—"

"Randy isn't the father." Mallory covered her face with her hands. "I can't believe this is happening. It was so stupid. *I* was so stupid."

Surprise filled Sabrina. She knew her sister and her high school boyfriend broke up at the beginning of the semester, but Sabrina just assumed…her sister hadn't acted interested in anyone else. During the last month every discussion she'd had with Mallory involved her begging Sabrina to go to some big church with her.

Mallory lowered herself onto the bathtub's edge. Sabrina watched as her sister rubbed her hands together; her expression filled with angst. "It was the first week of September. When I moved in here. We had a party." She shook her head and peered up at the ceiling. "I got totally wasted and ended up with a guy and—"

"Who?"

Mallory looked at her, tears brimming her eyes. Sabrina's heart broke, and she wished she could wipe away her sister's pain. "I don't even know his name. How awful is that?"

Sabrina couldn't take it any longer. She pushed away from the sink and wrapped her arms around Mallory. Her sister cried while Sabrina ran her fingers through long locks of hair. "It's going to be okay. I'm here for you."

As the words slipped from Sabrina's lips, dread filled her heart. It would be torture. Every day. Somehow she would get past the memories. She wouldn't turn her back on Mallory.

"This is why God tells us to stay pure till marriage. If only I'd known Him before…"

Sabrina blocked out her sister's words. She heard enough preaching at work from one of her workers. Since Mallory "found Jesus" a little over a month ago, that's all her little sister had wanted to talk about as well. But Sabrina didn't need a crutch, some wimpy faith to get her through life. She'd made a few bad choices in life. Dealt with the knocks that came with it. Dusted herself off and worked hard to achieve her goals. And she was happy with life. She lived it as she wanted.

A niggling of discontent poked at her heart when she thought of the last date she'd had. The one on her thirtieth birthday when the guy just assumed she'd want a nightcap. What she really wanted was to punch him square in the nose. Beyond that, she wanted to feel cherished and respected. But guys didn't seem to come that way these days.

Mallory discovered that the hard way. Maybe now she'd forget all this Jesus stuff and stop depending on something she couldn't see or touch. It wasn't as if God talked to Mallory. He obviously wasn't involved in her life since He allowed her to get pregnant after one silly mistake.

She said the one-night stand happened only a week after moving in, and wasn't it only a week or two after that that Mallory went all Holy Roller on her? That was proof enough that God didn't care about what was best for Mallory. She had the potential to be a terrific lawyer. Exceptional grades. Spunky personality. Natural bent toward fighting injustice. Where was God now? Obviously not here.

But Sabrina was. She was tangible. Mallory could depend on her, and Sabrina would help her sister. Whatever it took. She'd get her through school. Her sister was destined to be a lawyer, and Sabrina would see that it happened. God would have nothing to do with it.

"God's got a plan. He cares about every detail of our lives. Including your love life."

Brent Connors caught the basketball and tucked it under his arm as he and his childhood friend, Will White, walked to the bench. He grabbed his water bottle off the seat and took a quick swig. He really didn't want to listen to Will's counsel regarding his love life. Or lack thereof.

Several ladies had already arrived at the church's gymnasium for the zumba class that would start in the next few minutes. The quicker he could gather his things and get out of there, the better.

"Tell me you are not still whining over that teacher."

Brent glanced at Will's coworker from the factory. He had trouble liking the guy. Often negative and a bit pushy, but Brent knew Will tried to be a witness to Jason. Brent shook his head. "Nope. Haven't said a word about Ivy."

Saying her name aloud was like adding alcohol to an unhealed wound. At one time, he'd believed God had placed her in his life for a reason. To become his wife. Even her mother thought they'd make a perfect couple. But Ivy fell for a contractor. A guy with three kids, to boot.

"Take my advice, man. Stay single." Jason scratched his unshaven jaw. "My old lady harps on me all the time. Can't even walk through the door without her nagging about something."

Will nudged Jason with his elbow. "Maybe if you picked up your socks every once in a while."

Jason growled. "That's one complaint."

"Sounds like an easy fix," said Brent.

"Dude, you aren't married. You don't even know what it's like. You live alone."

Brent reached beneath the bench and grabbed his ball cap and car keys. He glanced at the door. Carrie Rice walked in and their gazes locked. He tried not to cringe as he watched her cheeks deepen in color. A few of her friends made it clear she had her sights set on Brent. And she seemed like a nice girl. A bit young, a full eight years his junior. Pretty, in a conservative, almost plain sort of way. Which he preferred. And she was a committed Christian and had been for years. Born and raised in the church. Which he required in a possible mate. But there was something there, or rather not there, that bugged him.

He focused his attention back on Jason and Will. Noting the gleam in Will's eye as he looked from Brent to Carrie, Brent shook his head to dissuade his friend from saying or doing anything to embarrass him. He looked back at Jason. "I don't know about married life, but I do live alone. And I do know about picking my socks up off the floor. Actually, a rather easy thing to do."

Jason huffed and turned toward Will. "I'll see you tomorrow at work, man. Brent, I'll see you next week."

"Later," said Will. Brent nodded to Jason.

Will grabbed his arm. "So, what do you think about Carrie?"

Brent scrunched his nose. "Seems like a nice girl. A little young."

"Tab says she likes you."

Brent chuckled when Will mentioned his wife. "What are we, in high school again?"

"No. But if you want me to, I'll ask her out for you."

Brent furrowed his brows and scowled at his friend. Realizing Will was teasing, Brent grinned. "Don't you think she's a bit short for me?"

Will shrugged. "Are we discriminating based on height? Just because she's around four foot ten, and you're about…"

"Six five."

"Only almost two feet. That's not too much."

"I'd have to pick her up to kiss her."

"So, you're already thinking of lip action?" Brent rolled his eyes, and Will punched his arm. "I'm just kidding. But don't decide against her based on that."

"I wouldn't."

"Hey, man. I've gotta go. Tab will have supper ready in ten minutes."

Brent glanced at the clock behind the gymnasium's sign-in desk. It was getting late, and he wanted to get home as well. He wouldn't tell Will, but he'd signed up for a Christian online dating service. His compatible matches should be posted.

He followed Will toward the door. His heartbeat sped up as he realized Carrie hadn't moved since she'd entered the building. He'd have no choice but to talk to her. He swallowed back the knot in his throat. Nodding toward her, he hoped she'd simply nod back and allow him to leave the gym. He started to push through the door.

"Hey, Brent."

He stopped at the sound of her voice. Will looked back, lifted his eyebrows, and grinned before heading outside. Brent pinched his lips as he turned back toward Carrie. He forced a smile. "Hi."

"I was wondering if you're going to Nat's next Friday."

Brent nodded. He'd been going to the church's singles' group outings since before Carrie was old enough to attend. Maybe not as much anymore since it seemed he'd become the senior citizen of the group. But Nat's fall party was always a lot of fun. "Yep."

She didn't say anything, and Brent knew she wanted him to offer to take her, but he didn't want to lead her on. Maybe he could like her, but standing next to her now felt uncomfortable. The girl's head barely reached his chest. Which was only part of the problem. The other part was that he thought of her as a girl, not as a woman.

Unsure what to do, he lifted his hand. "Well, I'd better be going. See you there on Friday."

Her expression brightened. "See you then."

Brent bit back his frustration that he'd managed to accidentally lead her on. He made his way to his car and cranked up the radio, allowing Casting Crowns's music to fill his heart and mind. Pulling into his driveway, his heart once again swelled with pride at the recent purchase of his first home. He'd saved for five years for the down payment. The modest log home on three acres had been a country dream come true. If God allowed, he would marry, raise a few kids, and die in this very house.

I'll just need to find me a simple, good Christian woman to share it with.

He walked inside and dropped his keys on the counter. Taking the leftover vegetable soup he'd made the day before from the refrigerator, he set the pan on the stove to warm. Having set up his home computer on the built-in desk across from the refrigerator, he plopped in the chair and turned on the computer.

God, I can hardly wait to see my matches. I just know You're about to show me the right woman for me. Maybe I'll even be able to see her for the first time tonight.

He logged onto the website, entered his user name and password, and waited for the information to load. One of the frustrating things about his home in the country was dial-up Internet.

Standing up, he walked to the stove and stirred the vegetable soup. He glanced back at the computer screen. Still loading. Trying not to feel anxious, he took a bowl out of the cabinet and a spoon from the drawer. He peeked again. Not finished yet. Taking the milk from the fridge, he poured a big glass and took a long swig. He placed the glass on the counter and looked at the computer screen.

Only one percent left. The green bar filled up to one hundred percent, and the screen changed. Brent blinked. *That can't be right.*

He sat in the chair and pushed the Refresh button on the website. The same screen popped up. Brent shook his head. It's not possible. There were supposed to be thousands of men and women on this website. *And I don't have a single match?*

Chapter 2

Sabrina sucked in a deep breath. She sat on the edge of the pleather seat, her shoulders straight and her hands clasped in her lap. She hadn't been in a gynecologist's office in eleven years. According to her friends, it was a carnal sin not to have a yearly checkup, but they had no idea what her last visit had been like. She had pushed it to the furthest recesses of her mind with no intention of retrieval.

And yet, after Mallory's announcement, she'd awakened almost every night this week, reliving the nightmare.

She watched as Mallory rubbed her hands together. An open-back, fabric gown draped her shoulders, her bare legs dangling from the end of the exam table. Mallory pulled her hair back in a ponytail, and for a moment, Sabrina saw her twelve-year-old sister waiting for her semiannual scoliosis checkup. At that time, their family's biggest fear had been that Mallory might have to endure back surgery and a change of lifestyle as a result of it. Seven years later and this doctor visit would most assuredly promise a life-style shift.

Mallory crossed her arms in front of her chest and rubbed her biceps with her hands. "I know it's stupid, but I'm kind of excited."

Not stupid. Feeling excitement was completely understood. Just not smart. Sabrina blinked and cleared her throat. Her sister needed to think with her head. Not her heart. "This is a big deal, Mal."

Mallory furrowed her brows. "I know that. It's practically the worst possible situation at the worst possible time, and yet, part of me is…excited. Did you know that the actual logistics of conception is a miracle in and of itself? It's like God personally forms the baby in the mother's womb."

Sabrina shook her head at her sister. She thought they were past this God stuff. Hadn't Mallory commented only a few days ago regarding how God could allow such a thing to happen? Sabrina hoped her sister would get her head out of the clouds and see logic and truth. And the truth was, if Mallory wanted to experience any success or happiness in life, she'd have to orchestrate it herself. Not depend on some higher power floating in the clouds. She parted her lips to say as much, but the door opened, and Sabrina clamped them shut.

The doctor, though balding on the top, sported light brown curls above his ears and along the base of his head. His eyes were a striking blue, despite being shielded by dark-rimmed glasses. Short and a bit plump, he was one of the oddest looking men Sabrina had seen, but he carried an air of calm confidence and sincerity that quelled Sabrina's butterfly-ridden stomach.

He extended his hand to Mallory then Sabrina. "I'm Dr. Coe. It's a pleasure to meet you both." He sat on the rolling, brown stool, and the material exhaled at his weight.

"Well, the pregnancy test was positive. According to the dates you gave the nurse, it appears your due date will be May 30. Everything seems to be fine, but we'll want to…"

His words jumbled together as remembrance shoved to the front of her mind, making her dizzy and nauseous. July 30 had been Sabrina's due date. At nineteen, she would have had to spend the entire summer fat and miserable. The notion had been repugnant. Incomprehensible. She wouldn't do it. No reason to do it. She was too young. Had too much going for her. The free clinic promised the procedure would be easy, relatively painless.

The room began to spin. Sweat beaded her forehead. Black closed in from the sides, the top, the bottom, and Sabrina felt herself slipping off the chair.

"Nurse!"

"Sabrina!"

Sabrina heard the doctor's and Mallory's voices blending into one sound. She felt a hand gripping her arm. A pungent odor burned her nostrils, and she pulled back her head and opened her eyes. Blinking, she swiped her forehead with the back of her hand and tried to pull herself back up on the chair with the other. "I'm sorry. I haven't eaten." A lie. She'd had lunch. A good one.

"It's okay, sweetie."

Sabrina looked up at the nurse. The white-haired woman handed her a juice box and a package of peanut butter crackers. Mallory stood on the other side of her, and Sabrina realized her baby sister had her hand wrapped around Sabrina's arm. "You scared the life out of me."

Sabrina forced a chuckle. "I'm fine. Just a little lightheaded."

"Well, I'm driving home." Mallory fished Sabrina's keys out of her purse. "You're going to sit in the passenger's seat and eat those crackers."

Sabrina didn't argue. She just wanted to get out of the doctor's office. To feel the crisp October air. To think of something besides doctor's visits and babies.

Mallory was quiet on the drive. Thankful for the silence, Sabrina nibbled a cracker and gazed out the window. She had a date Friday night. A blind date. If she thought about him and where they might go, she could push the memories back into the furthest recesses of her mind. The place where she'd kept them buried all these years.

She tried to think about what she could wear. Her black sweater with silver gemstones or the tight red blouse that accentuated her curves? She got a lot of compliments on her knee-high black boots, but that would mean she'd have to wear a skirt, and she wasn't sure if she wanted to wear one. Her sister missed the turn, and Sabrina looked at Mallory. Before she could ask, Mallory said, "I'm going to tell Mom and Dad."

Sabrina leaned her head against the headrest. "Do we have to do that today?"

"They'll get the doctor bill soon enough. Might as well be upfront now."

"You don't know how they'll respond."

Mallory rested her hand on Sabrina's leg. "It won't be so bad. You'll see."

Sabrina closed her eyes. No. It was Mallory who would see. She wrinkled her nose and pursed her lips, forcing the memories of how her parents had reacted to her "situation" to the back of her mind. A lot had happened in the last eleven years, and Mallory was their baby. Mom wasn't in public office anymore. Dad wasn't putting in quite as many hours at the office. Maybe things would be different.

Her sister pulled into the driveway and parked the car. Sabrina's heart pounded against her chest. The two-story, red brick colonial looked as pristine as ever. Beneath the second-story center window's balcony, a large wreath decorated with yellow, orange, and red foliage adorned the whitewashed door. The gardener had planted several yellow and white mums between the manicured shrubs along the front and around the three-tiered fountain that sat to the right of the house.

She forced one foot in front of the other as she followed her sister up the walk and into the immaculate house. Her parents' welcome was kind. Full of kisses and hugs and lighthearted reproof that their girls didn't visit often enough. *There's a reason for that.*

Sabrina bit her tongue to keep from saying anything she'd regret. It had taken a long time to become independent of her parents' pocketbook. Not an easy task for a girl with a shoe and purse fetish. But she'd done it, and she was glad to be on her own. Even so, she didn't want to fight with them in front of her sister, either.

Feeling overwhelmed, Sabrina sat at the end of the couch. The memories welled inside her again. She was nineteen. Not Mallory. She was standing where Mallory stood, pouring out her troubles. She was crying, confused, even though Mallory was calm and confident. Frustration with her parents mounted inside her.

"You're what?" her mother asked. The angry tone smacked Sabrina back into the present. Her mind had spun in so many directions she hadn't realized her sister had told them. She took in her mother's conservative navy blue suit. The perfect attire for a woman who'd spent two terms as a state representative, who still lobbied at the state's capital. She noted her neat, dark, bobbed hair. Her bright red lipstick, which always drew people to her winning smile—a smile that was nowhere to be found at the moment. Sabrina knew the words. The tone.

"Not you, too." The comment hissed through her father's lips with disdain and contempt. Sabrina had always been proud to tell friends that her daddy was a doctor; even though she'd wished he'd spent more time with her when growing up. Doctors were smart. They helped people. They were important. When she'd discovered her pregnancy eleven years ago, Sabrina believed it would be her father who would be her source of comfort. She'd been wrong.

"What have we done that both our daughters decide to get pregnant their first year of college?" The words, though asked to their father, had been directed at Mallory and Sabrina. Her mother walked away from them. She wrapped her arms in front of her chest and stared out the front window.

"What are you talking about?" Mallory furrowed her brow. She stared at Sabrina, a look of confusion and betrayal wrapped her features. Sabrina felt shame and embarrassment all over again. She wouldn't do this again. She was a successful woman. She was past that memory. Straightening her shoulders, she lifted her chin.

Mallory's chin quivered as she looked at Sabrina. "You were pregnant?"

Sabrina couldn't respond. It was never to be known. Never to be spoken again. She'd cried a million tears, lost days of sleep and over ten pounds. She hadn't made it through the semester. Dropped out. Had to start again fresh in the spring.

"Well, you're going to have to have an abortion," said their father.

Sabrina's ears burned. He'd said the same to her. Her stomach churned, and she feared the sole cracker she'd eaten would present itself again in unwanted form.

Mallory turned toward their dad. Sabrina noted the fight in her sister's stance. She wished she'd been that confident at her age. "I won't."

"You will," he responded.

Sabrina watched as their mother walked toward Mallory. She placed her hands on Mallory's shoulders. "Honey, think reasonably. You have such a bright future. You don't need this burden right now."

Mallory pulled away from their mother. "I won't abort my baby."

"Well, we won't pay for it," said their father.

"We'll take you off our insurance tomorrow, if need be." Their mother's words were tense, but she quickly exhaled and offered a smile. "Now, Mallory…"

Mallory straightened her shoulders. "I won't do it, Mom."

"Then, we have no option… ."

Sabrina couldn't take it anymore. The scene was too real. Too heart wrenching. Too familiar. Conjuring all the strength she could muster, she stood and grabbed Mallory's hand. "I'll help you, Mallory. Come on."

Her parents berated both of them as they walked out the door. Outside the car, Sabrina pulled her sister into a hug. Mallory's strong resolve broke, and tears raced down her cheeks. Sabrina sucked in her breath and swallowed, trying to keep her own emotions at bay.

Mallory sniffed as she pulled away. Her sister studied her, and Sabrina knew the questions were coming. She kissed the top of her sister's head. "I'll get you through this."

"You had an abortion?"

"No." Sabrina shook her head. "But I was going to."

Brent flopped onto the office chair and leaned back. He enjoyed volunteering as the director for the town's local food pantry, but he was glad to be back at work. This morning had been a difficult one at the pantry. For one, there had been a discrepancy between the number of vouchers and the amount of food that had been distributed. It had taken him a full hour before he found and fixed the error made by one of the new volunteers. And since the school system had the day off, he'd also spent the morning with Ivy and her stepdaughter.

Not quite a year had passed since Brent had hoped for a relationship with the elementary teacher. She was perfect for him. Naturally beautiful. A terrific personality. Spent her life living for the Lord. Even her mom thought they'd be a great match. But nine months ago, she decided to marry a local contractor/widower, take on his three children, and now she was pregnant with his child. Even had a five-month-along belly to prove it.

Brent put his hands behind his head, lacing his fingers and leaning back. He didn't want Ivy. Not now. He was happy for her. Truly and completely.

He wanted what she had. All of his friends were happily married. Most of them had a kid or two. He spent his days working with women, encouraging them to carry their unplanned babies to term, to consider adoption, or helping them learn how to be good parents. It was his turn. And he was ready.

God, You can deliver Your choice for me anytime. I'm ready. I'm willing. I'm anxious, even.

A knock sounded outside the office door. He jumped forward, his chair squeaking at the unexpected change in position. Grabbing the lip of the desk with one hand, he motioned with the other. "Come on in."

The red hair caught his attention first as Carrie gingerly opened the door. Her light green eyes begged pardon as she stepped inside. Brent grinned at the cellophane-covered paper plate in her hand. Though hesitant, she placed the plate on his desk. "Will told me chocolate chip cookies are your favorite, and since I made some, I thought I'd bring a few… ."

Her voice caught, and Brent watched as crimson raced up her neck and dotted her cheeks. Having mercy on her, he pulled back the wrap and grabbed a cookie. "They are my favorite."

He took a bite. It was the perfect consistency. Moist, but not mushy. Just the right amount of chocolate. He raised his eyebrows. "This may be the best chocolate chip cookie I've ever tasted."

Her cheeks deepened in color, and she clasped her hands in front of her as she nodded. "Thank you."

He watched as she stood quietly before him. From what he'd known of Carrie, she was a model of humility and grace. His compliment obviously pleased her, but she didn't try to play games or act coy or clever as he'd seen so many women do. Her blue jeans and green blouse were modest. Her makeup was simple, allowing the green in her shirt to enhance the color of her eyes. By all appearances, she was what he wanted in a wife. And yet, there wasn't a spark.

Maybe that comes with time, Lord. I was just telling You I'm anxious for a wife, then Carrie walks through my door.

His phone rang, and Brent lifted his index finger toward Carrie as he answered it. "Yes?"

"Your one o'clock is here."

"Okay. Send them on back."

He hung up the phone and shrugged. "My appointment is here."

Carrie lifted her hand. "No problem. I didn't plan to stay."

She reached for the door, and Brent grabbed her hand. "Thanks for the cookies. They are delicious."

After she walked out, Brent chewed on his lower lip. He should give her a shot. Take her out on a date. Just see what happened. Ready for his appointment, he picked up a pen to jot down notes as a girl walked into his office. She was young, obviously in her teens—hopefully, late teens—and quite the looker. The door opened wider and another woman entered.

Brent swallowed. The older version of the teen took his breath. Long, dark hair—straight and silky. Eyes the deepest brown he'd ever seen. Her bright red sweater hugged tight to her figure and the black skirt she wore barely touched the top of her knees. Long black boots accentuated the curve of her calves. Brent swallowed again. Gorgeous didn't cut it. Stunning wasn't good enough. Sinful described the woman best.

Trying to regain his wits, he sucked in a deep breath and inhaled her tantalizing scent. She was temptation incarnate.

Forcing himself to think with his mind and not his senses, he stood behind the desk and extended his hand to the younger woman. "I'm Brent Connors. It's a pleasure to meet you. I assume you're Mallory."

The teen nodded and shook his hand. She pointed to the other woman. "This is my sister, Sabrina."

Sabrina nodded and grabbed his hand. Brent felt as if she'd set it on fire. When she released him, he had to force himself not to flex his fingers. Instead, he motioned for them to have a seat. He sat and clasped his hands on top of the desk. "How can I help you?"

"I just found out I'm pregnant," said Mallory.

"Congratulations!" Brent said. He noted the scowl on Sabrina's face and cleared his throat. "Since you're here, I can only assume this is an unexpected pregnancy. But allow me to assure you that God doesn't make mistakes and that your baby has a purpose."

Mallory's expression brightened, but Sabrina pursed her lips and narrowed her gaze.

He pulled a few brochures out of plastic wall holders and handed them to Mallory. "I'm not saying things will be easy, but I am encouraging you to consider all your options."

Mallory shook her head. "I'm not considering abortion."

Brent nodded. "I'm glad to hear that. Did you want to discuss adoption or…"

She shook her head again. "No. I want to keep the baby. Sabrina has agreed to help me." She grabbed her sister's hand, but Sabrina's gaze remained focused on him.

"Okay. So how can I help?"

Mallory scrunched her nose. "I don't know. I guess I don't know where to start, what to ask, what to do. I'm a new Christian, and I don't know what it means to be a good mom, and I don't know how to pay for it."

He watched as Sabrina lasered her sister with a look of contempt. "I told you I would take care of that."

"I know, but it's not your job to do that. You're already giving me a place to stay. I have to step up and be responsible and…"

"We can talk about this at home." Sabrina's words sliced through gritted teeth.

Mallory shook her head. "No. I have to do this."

Before she could finish, Sabrina stood to her feet. She nodded to him then walked out of the office. Brent cleared his throat. He'd had people storm out of his office before, but this time his heart twisted with pain for Sabrina, instead of Mallory. He looked back at the teen. "How can I help you?"

"I need to know how to be a mom. In every way. And I need someone to talk to."

Brent smiled. The girl was young. He looked at his

paper with the information she'd filled out before their meeting. Only nineteen. But she was a fighter. And God would see her through. He stood and motioned toward the door. "I'll take you to Sandy's office. She'll be able to tell you about various services available to you—prenatal classes, financial advice, and more. Then we'll head back to the front and pencil you in another appointment with me."

"To talk?"

He nodded. "To talk."

She placed her hand on his arm. "This will sound kinda funny, but I can already tell I like you. I'm a good judge of character, you know."

Brent didn't say anything, but he couldn't help but wonder if she'd been a good judge of character regarding the baby's father and if that father was still in the picture.

"Will you do me another favor?"

He looked down at Mallory. "What?"

"Pray for my sister."

Brent pictured the beauty sitting in the seat across from his desk. He felt drawn to her in the most primitive of ways. He'd pray for her all right. Pray he wouldn't have to spend time with her. Temptation was written all over her.

Chapter 3

Sabrina squirted whipped topping in a circular pattern on top of the mocha frappé. She placed the clear plastic lid on top and pushed until it popped into place. As the financial manager of several of the popular, franchised coffee shops, it had been a long time since she'd worked behind the counter serving customers. It was relatively easy work. Mentally, anyway. And she needed something to keep her hands busy without overloading her mind.

"Here you go." She handed the cold drink to the woman who appeared to be a few years her junior. As the woman walked away, Sabrina admired the adorable cream-colored, lacy shirt. It was a terrific fit and the cut slimmed what Sabrina could tell was a bit-too-pudgy midsection. She wrinkled her nose. *But those worn-out red heels are atrocious.*

Looking back at the counter, she bit her bottom lip. The argument she'd had with her then-boyfriend, Josif, a few years ago niggled at her mind. He'd been disappointed by her critical views of others. Said it wasn't Christian-like. But was it her fault she'd been blessed with fashion sense and that it aggravated her to no end when people mismatched their clothes or wore things that were just plain tacky? He was her boyfriend, for crying out loud. She should have been able to vent petty annoyances to him without being accused of being some great big, ugly sinner.

She pulled her iPhone out of her apron pocket. Noting the time, she shoved the phone in her back jean pocket and took off the apron. She needed to run home and freshen up before her blind date that evening. How she hoped she liked the guy! Mallory had already moved into her spare room, and she needed an evening that didn't involve worrying over her little sister.

"You leaving?"

Sabrina looked at Gretchen and smiled. Although well into her fifties, she didn't look a day over forty. Though they were in different stages of life, Sabrina enjoyed her relationship with Gretchen. Only a decade ago, Gretchen had trained her in the fine art of coffee making. She'd comforted Sabrina on more than one occasion after the miscarriage. Even took a few of Sabrina's shifts when she was having a particularly emotional night. The woman always said she was praying for her, but Sabrina didn't want anything to do with God.

Time and hard work had healed Sabrina. And now Gretchen still worked behind the counter as a part-time employee who worked for fun, while Sabrina had moved up in the franchise's corporate world.

"Yep. Got a hot date tonight."

"Oh?"

"Blind date actually. Met him on the Internet. Saw a

picture, but you never know if that's truth or fiction." She nudged Gretchen with her elbow. "So, I'm hoping he's hot."

"I'm sure you'll have fun regardless."

Gretchen furrowed her brow as a troubled expression took over her features. Sabrina released a slow sigh as she prepared herself for the inevitable sermon. Feeling a bit vulnerable when she arrived to help out, she'd shared her sister's condition with Gretchen. A moment of weakness, to be sure.

Gretchen touched Sabrina's hand. "I'll be praying for you and your sister. Babies are such blessings, but they're hard work in the best of circumstances. And…"

Sabrina patted Gretchen's hands, hoping her friend got the message that she in no way, shape, or form wanted to speak about her own pregnancy situation when she'd first started working with Gretchen. It had been a moment of weakness that caused Sabrina to share the unplanned pregnancy with her coworker all those years ago. Something she had no intention of discussing again. "I appreciate that, but don't you worry. We'll manage just fine."

"God will take care of you. He knows exactly—"

"Thanks so much, Gretchen." Sabrina knew it was rude to cut her off, but she didn't want to hear about how God would take care of them. God had taken care of her eleven years ago. Let her miscarry her baby. Sure, she'd planned to abort, but she might have changed her mind. Losing the baby had been like nothing she'd expected. The mess. The pain. The emptiness. She'd been unprepared for the depression that followed.

She thought of her ex-boyfriend Josif. He'd been her only serious relationship since then. She bit back a chuckle. Wouldn't he have been shocked to learn of her sordid past? Especially after he'd turned Holy Roller on her. Accused her of not having a personal relationship with God.

Who did he think he was, judging her in such a way? She'd gone to church with him and his family every Sunday. She still attended church. A different one. On occasion. Okay, so maybe it had been a while, but did that really make her a bad person?

Slipping to the back office, she yanked her purse out of the desk drawer. She pulled out her keys and waved to Gretchen and the other employees as she headed out the door. Once in the car, she cranked up the radio and sang along to the latest pop song. Pulling into her driveway, she sighed in relief that Mallory's car wasn't there. Within half an hour, she'd changed outfits, freshened up her makeup and hair then headed toward town.

After parking in front of the restaurant where she'd agreed to meet Andy, she pulled out a tube of bright red lipstick and painted her lips the same color as her new acrylic fingernails. Her phone dinged, and she looked at her text. Andy sent a picture of himself already sitting in a booth. She raised her eyebrows. He was a very nice looking guy. Thick dark hair. Good, solid chin. Appeared athletic. In the picture, she couldn't make out if his eyes were blue or green, but it didn't really matter to her.

She flipped her hair over her shoulder. She looked good, too. He wouldn't be disappointed. She walked into the restaurant, spotted Andy in the corner, and walked toward him. He looked up, and she offered a shy wave.

The expression of pleasure that wrapped his features as he smiled was proof enough that she had been right. He approved of her looks. She offered her hand as she slid into the booth across from him. "I'm Sabrina. It's great to meet you."

"Andy." He took her hand then tilted his head. "The pleasure is mine." He blew out a breath. "This will sound awful, but I was worried about what you'd look like, but you're gorgeous. By far prettier than your picture."

Sabrina smiled and lifted her eyebrows to add just a bit of flirtation to the conversation. "You're not so bad yourself."

The waitress arrived and took their drink orders. Sabrina analyzed her date while he spoke to the woman. She noticed his gaze shifted to the door more often than she felt it should. As if he was expecting someone else. Who would he be expecting? She pushed the concern aside, deciding he was probably just nervous.

The waitress left, and Andy looked at her again. He smiled, and Sabrina couldn't help but admire his beautiful, white teeth. She'd been wrong about his eyes. They were actually brown. Light with a ring of green around his pupil. He placed his hand on hers. "So, tell me about yourself."

The gesture was a bit too personal for having only met moments before, and Sabrina maneuvered her hand out from under his. "I'm a financial manager for…"

She watched as his left thumb rubbed the bottom of his left ring finger. A gesture a man who normally wore a ring would do. She cocked her head. "Andy, how long have you been divorced?"

His face blanched, and he sat back against the booth. "I'm not divorced."

"Married?"

He opened his mouth and shook his head, but she saw the red streak crawling up his neck.

She grabbed her purse and jumped off the seat. "Sorry, Andy. I don't date married men."

He didn't respond and didn't follow her as she stormed back to her car. Proof enough her assumption was right. *So much for Internet dating.*

She gritted her teeth as she started the car. Gretchen's

promise to pray for her and her sister pounded against her brain. "Thanks for the nice evening out, God. I needed some time to relax. Unwind a little. But You don't seem to care too much about letting me experience any peace. It's all trials and tribulations."

Brent bowed his head as Will led the Bible study group in the closing prayer. God had spoken to his heart through the book of Romans this evening. Reminded Brent that He'd given him a purpose solely for him. That His plans for Brent were already in place.

He'd needed to hear that today. Most of his Friday had been spent doing paperwork in the office. He'd had only one counseling session. The girl, only sixteen, was set on having an abortion. Her boyfriend urged her to consider other options and was the one who'd set up the appointment. Brent was surprised by the kid. It wasn't often that the guy took such initiative. Especially at such a young age, only a high school junior.

Like always, Brent prayed before the session. But the girl had been unreceptive to anything he had to say. Nearing the beginning of her third month of pregnancy, Brent asked her if she'd like to hear the baby's heartbeat. She wouldn't consider it, and when the couple left, Brent felt failure weighing his shoulders. Failure that would probably result in the loss of that baby's life.

"Amen," said Will, and Brent and the other men echoed the word.

He scooped up his Bible and stood. Not wanting to head straight home, he said, "Anyone wanna grab a burger?"

Adam scratched at the furry red beard that wrapped his jawline. "Can't. Ate with the wife and kids two hours ago." He tapped his watch. "If I don't get home to help with bedtime, I'll be in a world of trouble."

"Same here," said Bernie. The new and youngest guy to their group was small and wiry and wore glasses that were too big for his face. Heart of gold, but he was the oddest character Brent had ever seen. *And even he's married with a new baby.*

He could spend more time with the singles' group at the church. They often ate out together or went on one adventure or another. There were times he did go places with them. And yet, he enjoyed the men's Bible study group, even if all of them were married. He felt so much older than most of the singles since the person closest to his age was twenty-four, almost five years younger.

The men started to walk out the door. Will grabbed Brent's hand in a firm shake. "I'm sorry, man. Wish I could." He raised his eyebrows. "You wanna come over and hang out for a while?"

Brent appreciated his friend's offer, but he knew Will worked long hours through the week. His wife, Tab, enjoyed their Friday nights. He pulled his keys out of his jeans pocket. "Nah. You go on home. I'll just grab a bite on the way."

After walking to the car, he got in, started it, and drove to his favorite burger joint. He shifted the gear into Park. *Another exciting Friday night of burger and fries by myself.*

He bit back a growl as he walked inside. He could have asked Carrie out. He'd had a lot of fun at Nat's party, and the woman had made it abundantly clear she was interested. But, he wasn't. He tried to be. Told himself on more than one occasion to just ask her out. Give it a shot. But he didn't want to lead her on, either.

After ordering his usual, he paid the cashier, waited for his food then turned with tray in hand to find a place to sit. The place was full. Not many seats to choose from. He spied a place toward the front of the restaurant. He paused when he saw the lone woman sitting in the booth across from the empty one. *Sabrina?*

The woman was dolled up in a fancy red shirt. Her dark hair fell in a shiny, straight mass down the front of her shoulder. She appeared ready for a fancy dinner. So why was she sitting alone at the burger joint?

His heart pounded against his chest. Mallory had asked him to pray for her sister. He'd enjoyed getting to know Mallory. The teen had stopped by on several occasions for snippets of advice or information regarding her pregnancy. She'd made quick friends with the receptionist, and he'd noticed the two of them often had lunch together, since Mallory's break between her college classes fit with Vanessa's schedule.

Sabrina looked upset. Surely she hadn't been stood up. She wasn't his type, but he couldn't deny the woman was gorgeous.

"Why don't you go sit with her?"

He swallowed at the Spirit's prompting. That was the last thing he wanted to do. First, he didn't want her to think he was interested. Second, she may have a date coming. Third, it would embarrass him to just walk up to her and say *you look a little lonely. May I join you?* And fourth... he couldn't think of a fourth.

"Just ask her."

Swallowing hard, heat rose up his cheeks as he made his way to the front of the restaurant. He could just turn around, ask the cashier to bag it up, and go home. The idea was tempting, but the nudging of the Spirit was stronger.

He made it to the edge of the table. She looked up, a scowl wrapping her features. *So much for a warm welcome.* He forced himself to smile as he nodded across from her. "Mind if I join you?"

She narrowed her gaze and stared at him. He started to turn on his heels to make good on his idea to bag up his dinner when she nodded. "Why not?" She pointed to the booth. "Have a seat."

Definitely not an ego-booster kind of woman, but Brent slipped in across from her. He opened his straw, put it in his soft drink then took a long swallow. Sabrina's gaze never veered from his face. She seemed to measure him up, to see if he was worthy of sitting across from her.

Praying God would give him the strength to be a good witness, he unwrapped his burger and met her gaze with his own. "I'm enjoying getting to know your sister."

Her hard expression softened a bit, and Brent realized she cared deeply for Mallory. "She's a good kid." She twisted the napkin in her hands. "I'm glad she's keeping the baby."

"Me, too."

"I'll do anything to help her." She looked toward the window, her eyes seeming to stare past the parking lot, past the street, into a world of its own. "It's going to be hard."

"Babies aren't easy." He took a bite of his sandwich and wiped his mouth.

"You're not married, are you?"

Brent swallowed the bite as he shook his head.

She looked down at her fries. She picked one up, dipped it in ketchup then put it in her mouth. "Just making sure."

Brent grinned, wondering what she meant by that response. She looked up at him. Her right eyebrow rising higher than the other as she smiled back. "The last guy who sat across from me was married." With both hands, she patted the booth on each side of her. "Which is why I'm here."

Brent wrinkled his nose. "Guess you didn't know?"

"Not a clue. Until I was sitting across from him and he

was watching the door and twirling an imaginary ring on his left hand." She released an exasperated sigh. "Why are guys such jerks?" She cocked her head. "It's Brent, right?"

He nodded. "Yes. It's Brent. And not all guys are jerks."

She pursed her lips. "So says a guy."

"I'll have you know that I want very much to find a woman, get married, and be faithful to her."

He bit the inside of his cheek. Why had he just said all that? That sounded a whole lot like a come-on. He didn't know this woman, and she was nowhere near his type.

She raised her right eyebrow again as she leaned forward across the table. The soft scent of her perfume wafted to his nose, and he tightened his stomach muscles at the tantalizing scent. The mystery in her dark eyes drew him, and he found himself fighting not to stare at her lips. "So why haven't you?"

"God hasn't brought the right woman, yet."

She leaned back in the booth and blew out an exasperated breath. "If I hear one more thing about God, I'm going to hurl." .

Brent blinked and sucked in a deep breath. He scooped up the hamburger and took a much-too-big bite. He had no idea what just happened. Nothing he could explore, even if he wanted to. Sabrina wasn't a Christian, but he would be praying for her.

Chapter 4

Brent woke up early and headed to his parents' house. It had been three weeks since his dad's knee replacement surgery. Though his father was healing nicely, he still had no business trying to do yard work. And Brent knew the huge oak trees in his parents' yard had to have shed most of their leaves, meaning the yard would need some work. And if he didn't get over there soon enough, his dad would try to take care of it.

He drank in the beauty of Tennessee's mountains as he made his way along the winding roads leading to the farmhouse. He couldn't imagine a place on earth more beautiful than the small community of Greenfield during fall. Nestled in the heart of the Smoky Mountains, they were surrounded by God's palette of the perfect mixtures of blues, greens, and browns. At this time of year, He added oranges, yellows, and reds of every shade imaginable. Brent never tired of seeing God's changing colors on this land.

He pulled into the driveway. As he expected, his dad was outside. Thankfully, he was still sitting on the front porch swing. Brent hopped out of the car and made his way up the walk. "Whatcha doin' outside, Dad?"

Though fifty-eight, his dad still had most of his hair, which hadn't even changed color much. His green eyes twinkled with mischief, and Brent knew he'd showed up just in time.

His mom opened the screen door. She wiped her hands on a dishcloth. Unlike his dad, his mom's hair was almost fully gray. Still long, she wore it in a high ponytail, the same style she'd had for as long as he could remember. Her blue eyes were striking and her skin still smooth, making her look younger than she was, even with the graying hair. She pointed to the yard. "He was getting ready to try to get on that lawn mower to collect those leaves. I told him I'd put him over my knee and spank his rear end like a little child if he even thought of trying."

Brent grinned, and his father winked back at him. His mom had threatened to spank their father for as many years as he remembered her wearing a ponytail. She loved her family something fierce and would fight a mountain lion barehanded if necessary to ensure they were safe and healthy. Brent's dad seemed to enjoy doing things to threaten his own safety and would often get her riled up.

Brent crossed his arms in front of his chest. "Dad, you're not raking those leaves."

"I can help."

His mother clicked her tongue. "Oh no, you won't. You'll sit yourself right here." She touched Brent's arms, stood on tiptoe, and kissed his cheek. "I'm glad you came, son. You'll stay for lunch, won't you?"

I don't have anything else to do. He bit back his frustration and smiled. "Of course."

"Good." She patted his arm. "I'll fix up something special."

"Hmph," his father growled. "I guess I'm not worth fixing something special for."

His mother swatted the air. "Oh hush. You're fed every day, aren't ya?"

Brent chuckled as he hopped off the porch and headed for the shed. His parents bantered back and forth over the silliest things for a good part of the day, but he couldn't count the times he'd seen his father pick a wildflower for his mother and leave it on the windowsill before dinner or the times his mother had filled a glass of ice water and placed it on the nightstand just before his father headed to bed to read one of his hunting magazines. The love he'd seen between the two of them was one of the reasons he longed for the same thing.

Sabrina's face drifted into his mind as he opened the shed door. The sparkle in her eyes when she'd asked why he hadn't gotten married had haunted him last night. He hadn't been able to get the light scent of her perfume from his mind, either. It meant nothing. He knew it was just because he'd promised to pray for her. And pray for her was what he did most of the night.

He attached the leaf bag to the mower, maneuvered it out of the shed then hopped on and started it up. It wouldn't take long to get the job done, and it wouldn't take a strenuous effort, but his dad had no business sitting on the mower with his knee bent and jerking up and down as the machine made its way around the yard.

His mind shifted to the sixteen-year-old girl and boy he'd talked with yesterday. He wondered if the girl had changed her mind. He'd prayed for her as much as Sabrina. The list of families willing to adopt babies was unbelievable. He prayed she'd at least give the child the opportunity to be adopted.

Finished with the front yard, he guided the mower to the back. He'd call the boyfriend on Monday. His gaze took in the family's pond in the distance. He loved the fall, but he sure missed going out to the pond to catch fish. After a particularly difficult day at work, he often drove out and sat by the cool waters to allow his mind to unwind. In his mind, the wife God had picked for him would enjoy fishing as well.

He pursed his lips as an image of Sabrina wrinkling her nose at the fishing bait filtered through his mind. He shook his head. Why would he think that? The woman was nothing, not the first thing, like what he wanted in a wife.

He preferred natural beauty. Though he believed Sabrina was naturally beautiful, she seemed to enjoy caking the paint on her face. Her hair was dark as night. Gorgeous. No doubt about that. But he'd always envisioned himself with a blond-haired gal. Her clothes left little to the imagination, and he couldn't deny he wouldn't mind his wife having a figure like Sabrina's. But she was also cynical. Worldly. And most important, not a Christian.

Which is why she is completely wrong for me.

He remembered the trace of vulnerability he'd seen in her eyes before she'd stormed out of his office the first day he'd met Mallory. Having spent years working with women, teens, and couples who'd found themselves in unplanned pregnancies, he couldn't help but wonder at Sabrina's response. Had she been in the same predicament? She obviously didn't have any children. But had she had a child? Given one away? Aborted a baby?

He shook his head at the idea. God forgave every sin. Every one—from lying to cheating, to stealing, to killing. Every one. Still, the thought of Sabrina having been pregnant and terminating her pregnancy felt like a stab to the heart then a twist of the knife just to ensure the full amount of pain.

Realizing he'd finished the backyard, he drove to the shed, emptied the leaves into trash bags, and put away the mower. He walked around to the front. His dad had already gone inside. Brent slipped off his boots on the porch and walked into the house.

"Wash your hands. I've got lunch ready," his mom called from the back of the house.

"Okay," Brent hollered back. His dad reclined on the couch, his recovering leg propped up on pillows. "Feeling a little sore, Dad?"

"A little."

Brent pinched his lips together. That meant his dad was hurting.

"Don't worry." His dad smiled, but Brent could tell it didn't reach his eyes. "Your mom gave me some medicine."

Brent nodded as he headed to the downstairs bathroom to wash up. He wondered what his father had tried to do before he'd arrived. There was no telling. A person had to practically tie him to the couch to get him to sit still. Once cleaned, he headed back to the living area. His mom set up TV trays so they could eat together. Brent knew she wouldn't eat at the table as they always had without his dad joining them.

His mom stood over his father, fluffing the pillows behind him. "Go ahead and sit down, Brent. I've made your favorite. Fried pork chops. Mashed potatoes. Green beans. And biscuits."

"She never cooks for me like that," whined his father.

"Oh hush." His mother swatted his arm, but Brent noticed she barely touched him. *Must be trying not to jostle him much.*

Brent sat in a chair across from his dad. "I know Mom spoils you all the time."

His dad winked and placed his index finger to his lips. When Mom walked out of the room, he whispered, "I know that, but an old man's gotta keep the spark alive somehow."

Brent shook his head. "You and Mom are crazy."

"Crazy about each other. And have been for going on forty years."

Brent chewed the inside of his cheek. He'd felt ready to settle down long before most of his buddies had. Maybe it was because Will and Tab married in high school, and Will had been his best friend since they were old enough to walk. Maybe it was because he wasn't all that interested in parties or dating. Will used to say he was an old fuddy-duddy at heart. Whatever it was, by the time he was twenty-three, he was ready to get married.

Five years had passed. Both of his older sisters were married with three kids a piece. All of his friends had taken the plunge. He was the only one left. And no prospects. Well, except Carrie.

And Sabrina.

He blinked and shook his head. What was he thinking? Sabrina was all wrong. In every way. He pushed the thought as far away as possible. Maybe he just needed to focus on Carrie. Or maybe he should try another Internet site. Surely he'd have more possible matches than last time. At least one.

Sabrina gritted her teeth as she followed her sister and some girl she'd met at ProLife Pregnancy Center into the church. It wasn't as if she never went to church. She did. But it had been a while, and she hadn't planned on it anytime soon. Lately, it seemed God had been working directly against her.

Having Mallory move into her house hadn't been too difficult. Since their parents had always provided for all of Mallory's needs and wants, her sister didn't have a job, which meant that after school she cleaned, washed laundry, went to the store, and cooked. It was wonderful. On the flip side, she didn't have a job, and their parents weren't giving her money anymore, which meant Sabrina was footing the bill.

Thankfully, they hadn't taken Mallory off their medical insurance. Sabrina knew they wouldn't. The risk of scandal would be too great. She could just see the headlines: "Past Representative Kicks Pregnant Teen Daughter to the Curb." She had no doubt her parents feared the headline, and that was probably the sole reason Mallory was able to get proper medical care.

Mallory grabbed her hand. "Come on. I like to sit in the front."

Sabrina dipped her chin and glared at her sister. "You're kidding, right?"

"Not kidding. Come on."

Mallory started to pull her forward, and Sabrina yanked back her hand. "I can walk." She lifted her shoulders and chin and made her way to the front of the building. She didn't look around. Hoped there wasn't anyone there she knew. The church was ginormous, so most likely, there was a plethora of past and present customers.

She kept her eyes focused on the front as she made her way to the second row of seats. The front of the church looked more like a stage than a platform for a preacher to stand on. There was a pulpit, but it was clear and was set to the side. Several musical instruments splayed across the front—three guitars, a keyboard, and drums. Two huge screens hung on the front left and right sides of the building. A wave of nostalgia washed over her. The place reminded her of the church she'd attended for years with Josif's family in Gatlinburg.

Now, she avoided the city for any reason except to take care of the coffee shops she had to tend. A few months after Josif married Mirela, Sabrina moved, ironically, to the town where Mirela was from. But the move had made sense. It was the exact central location of the shops she managed. She never had to drive more than forty-five minutes to get to work. And it was closer to her hometown, closer to Mallory's community college—which, as luck would have it, turned out to be very convenient.

She sat down beside Mallory then placed her purse in the seat beside her. She looked at her sister. "So, this is where you've been going to church?"

Mallory shook her head. "No. This is Vanessa's church. I've been going to the one on First Street, but since…"

Her sister's voice caught, and Sabrina narrowed her gaze. "Since what?"

Mallory shrugged, but Sabrina knew something was wrong. "I just thought since I've made such good friends with Vanessa I'd try her church."

Sabrina furrowed her brow. "You're not telling me the whole truth." Sudden dawning hit her in the face. "Was someone mean to you because you're pregnant?"

Mallory pursed her lips. "Now, Sabrina, you know that people in the church are just as imperfect as people in the world. There are always going to be people—"

"I knew it." Sabrina's heartbeat raced, and her blood ran hot. She fanned her face with the bulletin some boy had given her when she walked in the door. Grabbing her purse, she decided she would not stay here another moment. Churchgoers were hypocrites with a capital *H*. She'd seen her fair share of Christians who didn't act the same on Monday as they had at church the day before. She was just as bad as they. Sitting in a chair at the front of a church when she had no desire to be there. What had God ever done for her?

She turned and started to stand when her face bumped into a chest covered with a white button-down shirt. She gasped and stepped back. "I'm sorry."

"My fault."

"Brent!" Mallory squealed, pushed past Sabrina, and wrapped her arms around the towering man.

Sabrina hadn't realized how tall he was. Of course, every time she'd seen him, he'd been sitting, but still— the man stood a full foot above her head. He was thinner than most of the men she dated, but she could tell he had the build of a basketball player.

She blinked. What was she thinking? The men she dated? Brent Connors would be the last man on the planet she would date. A Goody-Two-shoes-Holy-Roller with a side of let's-pray-before-we-eat. No. He was definitely not the kind of guy she wanted to date.

He pointed to the chair beside her. "You mind if I sit with you all?"

"Well, I…" Sabrina wanted to leave. She didn't want him to join them. Unless it was to go back to the burger joint where she'd last seen him. That place had great hamburgers.

"Sure," Mallory said.

He waved at Mallory's friend. The girl waved back as he sat in the chair that had held Sabrina's purse only moments before. With an inner growl, Sabrina lowered back to the seat. She couldn't leave now. It would be rude. She'd have to pick up Mallory anyway once it was over. And what real excuse would she have?

Before she had time to sit back, music blared from speakers from every direction in the building. Sabrina smacked her chest with her hand. She hadn't even noticed the musicians walk on stage. Mallory hopped up on her left side. Brent stood on her right. She clamped her mouth shut as she slowly stood between them.

The music to "Open the Eyes of My Heart" peeled from the instruments. Within seconds, three ladies began singing the chorus. The tune laced its way through her heart. Years ago she'd enjoyed the song. Didn't fully understand it, but she'd liked the melody.

Brent sang loud beside her. He had a terrific voice. A tenor, even though he sometimes shifted to baritone. She wanted to sing along with him. She knew the words. She even thought their voices would blend well. But she couldn't do it. She wouldn't. *Open the eyes of my heart, Lord?* If those lyrics didn't sound like the words of a desperate person, she didn't know any that did. She was not weak. She didn't need God.

Chapter 5

Brent couldn't stop thinking about her. He tried to tell himself it was because she needed prayer. She needed to accept Jesus as her Savior. And those things were true. But he also knew he was attracted to her. Desperately. Standing beside her in church had been torture. Her scent, whatever perfume she wore, drew him like a bee to nectar.

He placed another can of green beans on the food pantry's shelf then recorded the total number of cans on the spreadsheet. The pantry was well-stocked with vegetables, but they'd need to ask the area churches to start collecting canned meats again. With Christmas less than two months away, the schools might be willing to conduct a food drive as well.

The bell to the front door dinged, and Brent walked to the front of the building. Carrie stood in the doorway. Her red hair was pulled up in clips on both sides. She wore blue jeans, brown boots, and an emerald long-sleeved shirt that brought out the green in her eyes. She looked cute, natural. She was the kind of woman he should be attracted to.

Realizing she held several plastic bags in both hands, he took them from her and put them on the counter. "What's all this?"

Her cheeks darkened, and he couldn't deny he found her nervousness around him endearing. "Tab said you told Will you were low on canned meats, so everyone in our Bible study group went through their cabinets."

Brent nosed through the bags. There must have been thirty or more cans of tuna, ravioli, and vienna sausages. He looked back at her and smiled. "This is great."

She played with the cross pendant that hung from a gold chain around her neck and shifted her weight from one foot to the other. "It's not much, but…"

Brent couldn't stand seeing the poor girl act so anxious. He motioned for her to follow him then scooped up the bags. "You wanna help me stock the shelves?"

She brightened, and Brent noticed a dimple in her left cheek when she smiled. "Sure."

He took her several aisles back and showed her the different canned meat sections. "Pretty easy to figure out. Since they're all labeled."

"I think I could handle it."

"Are you saying you'd like to volunteer? One of my best workers is getting ready to have a baby and probably won't be coming back."

He didn't mention that only a year ago, he'd thought that particular volunteer would be a terrific candidate for the still vacant position of Mrs. Connors. After her wedding, Brent had been surprised that Ivy continued to volunteer at the food pantry. Her husband, Carter, knew Brent had been interested in her romantically. Ivy knew as well. Her mother had even picked Brent as the better choice. But Ivy had chosen Carter and continued to volunteer since she loved the work. Carter or one of his kids often came with her. Brent didn't mind, but the whole situation had been a bit awkward.

"We'd have to schedule around my work hours, but I'd love to volunteer."

"Great." Having placed the last can on the shelf and documenting the donation on the spreadsheet, he guided her to the office. "You'll have to fill out an application. We'll have to do a criminal check as well. Standard procedure."

She placed her hand on her chest. "Shew. That makes me feel better."

Brent furrowed his brow. "What do you mean?"

She smacked her hand against her thigh. "Now I know you're not a criminal decked in"—she lifted both her hands and made quotation mark gestures—"nice guy clothes." She elbowed him. "Get it?"

The goofy expression on Carrie's face tickled Brent, and he laughed. He raised both his hands in surrender. "Don't worry. I'm not a criminal."

"That's good to know, 'cause criminals come cute as well."

Brent crossed his arms in front of his chest and leaned back on his heels. "Does that mean you think I'm cute?"

Carrie's face blanched. She opened her mouth then shut it again. She averted her gaze, and Brent felt bad that he'd embarrassed her. He'd liked it when she'd acted like herself. He grabbed an application and handed it to her. "I'm getting ready to pick up some frozen foods at the grocery. You wanna go with me?"

She shook her head. "I'm sorry. I can't." She lifted the paper. "I'll get this back to you soon." She turned on her heels and walked out the door.

Brent sat in the office chair and plopped his elbows on

the desk. Intertwining his fingers, he chewed the inside of his cheek. He hadn't meant to run her off. He thought they were getting along pretty well. *There must be something about me that repels women. I'm like the female antimagnet.*

He leaned back in the chair, the old springs complaining against the shift in weight and movement. He didn't think he was that difficult to be around. Maybe not the best looking guy in the world. Definitely not the richest. But he was okay in the looks department, made enough money to live comfortably, and he was a nice guy. He knew Carrie was interested, but the first time he tried to flirt a bit, she raced out the door.

His iPhone sang "Amazing Love." He pulled it out of his pocket and saw that the center's receptionist, Vanessa, was calling. He frowned. She'd have no reason to call him on a weeknight. Pushing the button, he said, "Hello."

"Brent, I'm so glad you answered. I can't get hold of anyone, and my car is in the shop, and she called me a half hour ago crying. You gotta come get me."

Brent leaned up in the chair. "Whoa. Slow down, Vanessa. What are you talking about?"

"Mallory. Something's wrong with the baby. Sabrina took her to the hospital. My car is in the shop. She was going to take me to get it in the morning…"

"Tell me your address. I'm coming." Brent's heartbeat raced as he drove to Vanessa's house. Mallory's pregnancy may have started under difficult circumstances, but she was excited about the baby, and God had already used that unborn life to bring Sabrina to church.

"God, I pray for Mallory and that precious baby. You already know the circumstances. I pray that everything is all right, and Mallory will carry the baby to term, but I know You are sovereign. No matter what, use this to draw Sabrina to You."

He pulled into Vanessa's driveway, and she ran out of the apartment and jumped in the car. He halfway listened as Vanessa relayed everything Mallory had said to her before heading to the hospital. He prayed for Mallory and the baby, that nothing was wrong. His mind kept drifting to Sabrina, offering short prayers that she would see God's hand in this. Whatever the outcome.

After parking in the hospital parking lot, he and Vanessa hopped out and raced into the emergency room. Vanessa talked to the unit clerk while he scanned the room. A family on his left. A young man and an older woman beside them. A boy at the vending machine. Then he spied Sabrina on his right. She sat on the edge of the seat, her elbows on her knees, her face in her hands. Her shoulders jerked, and he knew she was crying.

After moving toward her, he lowered himself into the seat beside her. Touching her back, he whispered, "How can I help?"

She startled and looked up at him.

"I'm sorry." He pulled back his hand, and for a moment thought she would give him a good tongue-lashing.

Her eyes held such sadness. He wanted to wrap his arms around her and promise everything would be all right. That God cared for her sister more than any of them would ever know. But she didn't know God. Couldn't understand His peace.

She leaned toward him then buried her face in his chest. Surprised, but moved to the core of his being, he shifted and wrapped his arms around her. While she cried into his shirt, he begged God to save her.

Sabrina gripped the front of Brent's shirt. Past and present collided in her mind. The memories threatened to strangle her. All the while fear for her sister and her precious niece or nephew wrapped around her like a cocoon she couldn't break free from.

Her stomach cramped, twisted in knots as it had all those years ago. A picture of Mallory lying on the couch flashed through Sabrina's mind. Her little sister's face twisted with pain. She'd held her stomach and cried.

A decade-old memory surged through her. Sabrina remembered the blood. The final sign of the miscarriage. She had freaked out. Sobs had overtaken her as she tried to clean up enough to get to the hospital. No one had gone with her. She'd called her mom, but she hadn't shown up.

Only hours ago, Mallory had walked out of the bathroom, her face the color of snow. "I'm bleeding."

With the utterance of those two words, Sabrina whisked her into the car and headed straight for the emergency room. While Mallory cried on the phone to her new friend, Sabrina took long breaths, resolving to stay strong. Not to show weakness. Not to show fear.

The nurse wouldn't let her go back with Mallory. She didn't fight it. Her strength was waning. Tears were beginning to pool in her eyes.

She gripped Brent's shirt tighter. It was already wet beneath her cheek. His arms felt good wrapped around her. Strong and sure. He patted her back, and for a moment, she worried that he'd think her weak. Right now, it didn't matter.

Her toes curled in her shoes as she remembered how cold her feet had been during the D & C, the procedure to clean her uterus of the pregnancy her body had rejected. She thought the machine had sucked out and scraped every organ inside her body once the doctor had finished. When he left, she felt a part of her had been taken away. A part she still hadn't gotten back.

"Sabrina Moore."

Sabrina pulled away from Brent's embrace at the sound of her name. She swiped at her eyes with the back of her hands, thankful she'd already taken off her makeup. She looked up at the nurse, her heart filled with a mixture of hope and dread. "Yes?"

The woman's face was impossible to read, and her body language remained passive as she gestured for Sabrina to follow her. "Your sister would like to see you."

She made her way to the woman. When the door shut behind her, she realized she hadn't thanked Brent and Vanessa for coming. She'd take care of that later. Right now she had to focus on Mallory. No matter what.

Her stomach churned and her legs weakened as she thought of the possibility of her little sister enduring a miscarriage. Labor would be worse, and then there would be a child to take care of. But wouldn't the baby be a blessing? The miscarriage had left Sabrina feeling empty, hopeless. Broken.

Please, God. Please, let her be okay.

The rational part of her mind chastised her for calling out to God. It was weakness. A show of desperation. But she was desperate. And she'd do anything to protect her sister.

The nurse pushed open a door. Terrified, Sabrina balled her fists and walked inside. Mallory lay on the bed, a blanket on top of her. Sabrina relaxed her hands and exhaled when she noted the smile on Mallory's face. A young, light-haired nurse stood beside her, and a doctor sat on a chair at Mallory's feet. The man appeared barely old enough to have made it through college, let alone medical school. He motioned her inside. "Your sister was quite adamant that you see this."

Sabrina made her way to Mallory and grabbed one of her sister's hands. The black monitor beside the bed came to life, and Sabrina gasped when she saw the gray image on the screen. She pointed. "Is that… ?"

Mallory nodded. Tears trailed down her cheeks. "My baby."

Sabrina bit her bottom lip as she drank in the view of the head, the body, the tiny arms and legs. A person had already formed in her little sister's womb, and she wasn't even showing yet.

"See that blinking?" The doctor placed a cursor of sorts over the baby's chest. "That's his heartbeat. Or hers."

Sabrina looked at the doctor. "So everything is okay?"

He turned toward Sabrina. "As I've told your sister, some spotting during pregnancy is not atypical. She needs to follow up with her obstetrician tomorrow. But from the looks of things"—he pointed to the screen—"everything appears fine."

"Thank God," whispered Sabrina.

"That's what I said. Exactly."

Sabrina looked back at her sister. She bit back a reprimand that her sister needed to stop depending on a being she couldn't see. Sure, Sabrina had prayed to Him in a moment of desperation. But that proved her point. People seek God when they have nowhere else to turn.

She turned toward the doctor. "Thank you for your help."

"No problem."

His smile was warm as he stepped closer to her. He took off his gloves and offered his hand. Sabrina noticed he wasn't wearing a wedding ring. Up close, she realized he looked more mature than he had at first glance. Out of habit, her hand went up to her hair, which was tied in a knotted ponytail at the top of her head. She remembered she wasn't wearing makeup and cringed. Her eyes were probably swollen as well. He opened his mouth to say something then stopped himself, nodded, and walked out of the room.

Mallory giggled. "I think he wanted to ask you out."

Sabrina swatted the air. "Don't be silly."

Mallory shrugged. "I don't know."

The nurse chuckled. "Well, he is brand new to the community. All the single nurses are after him."

"You, too?" asked Mallory.

She held up her left hand. "Nope. I'm married." She pointed to Mallory's clothes in a bag on the counter. "I'll let you help Mallory, since you're here. Let me know when you're finished. I'll take her to your car in the wheelchair."

"What?" Mallory asked.

"Standard procedure."

Sabrina nodded. When the nurse shut the door behind her, Sabrina helped Mallory out of the bed. "Brent and Vanessa are in the waiting room."

Mallory sighed. "She's been such a good friend. God's really blessed me."

Sabrina didn't respond as she handed Mallory her shirt.

"You've really been there for me, Sabrina. I appreciate it."

"Of course, I'll be there for you. You're my sister."

Mallory didn't respond as she slipped into her sweatpants. Sabrina helped her into her tennis shoes and tied the laces so she wouldn't have to bend over. "I think I'm going to stay put on the couch until I can get in to see the doctor."

"That sounds like a good idea."

With Mallory dressed, Sabrina stood and headed toward the door.

"Whenever you're ready to talk about what happened, I'm ready to listen."

Sabrina sucked in a deep breath at Mallory's words. She knew what her sister was referring to. The miscarriage. Her desperate fear for Mallory must have been obvious, despite her efforts to hide her true feelings. *I didn't hide them from Brent, that's for sure.* Her cheeks warmed when she thought of her breakdown in the waiting room.

She shook her head. She couldn't talk about the miscarriage. It hurt so much. Right now, her little boy or girl would be ten and a half years old. In the fifth or sixth grade, depending on if Sabrina had chosen to send the child to kindergarten the very next month after his or her fifth birthday.

Looking at Mallory, she said, "Why don't we worry about you and keeping you healthy?"

The nurse arrived with a wheelchair, and Mallory sat down. They made their way through the automatic doors leading to the waiting room. Vanessa and Brent jumped up out of their seats.

Sabrina noted the damp spot on Brent's shirt where she'd cried against his chest. His gaze held hers, and she knew he wanted to know that she was all right. The intensity of his look stirred something within her, and she looked away. "I'll get the car."

She nodded at Brent then passed by him without a word. She felt his gaze on her back and hoped he wouldn't follow her. Wouldn't ask questions. Once she'd made it outside, she knew he'd decided to stay with Mallory. She was glad. He was the last person she wanted to talk to.

Chapter 6

Brent leaned over the food pantry desk, his elbows propped up on top and his hands cupping his face. He'd hardly slept the last two nights with the burden he felt for Sabrina and her sister. Vanessa told him Mallory was on bed rest for a while, and he had planned to call, but the feel of Sabrina wrapped in his arms, crying, still sent his thoughts into a tailspin.

"I finished checking for expired items."

Brent jumped up, and Carrie took a step back. "I'm sorry. Is everything all right?"

"I'm fine." He pressed the tips of his fingers against his temples and rubbed in a circular motion.

"Do you have a headache? I've got some ibuprofen in my purse."

Carrie's concern for him warmed his heart. He smiled. "Just haven't slept well the last few nights." He stretched his arms in front of him then looked back at her. Carrie looked cute in a brown and green jumpsuit of sorts. She had her hair pulled up in a ponytail. A few strands of her light red hair had come loose around the base of her neck. "You've worked hard. You wanna grab a bite to eat?"

She clasped her hands, wringing them together. "I'd love to, but I'm already meeting some friends tonight."

"No problem." He looked back at the desk. For a girl who was supposed to be head over heels for him, he certainly couldn't get her to agree to go anywhere with him. And he needed her to help him get his mind off Sabrina. The motive was a selfish one, but he hoped his feelings for Carrie might develop if he spent time with her. She was young, but Carrie was the exact kind of girl he planned to marry.

"But I'm free tomorrow."

Brent looked back at her. She smiled, exposing the adorable dimple in her left cheek. She really was cute. He nodded. "Okay. How 'bout seven o'clock?"

"Sounds good." She took her purse off the hook behind the door then waved. He noticed the blush spreading across her cheeks. "Bye, Brent."

"Bye."

She left the office, and he heard the front door's bell ding as she opened and shut it. He turned off the laptop and closed it. His stomach twisted with the thought of taking Carrie to dinner the following night. He wasn't attracted to her in the same way he was Sabrina. Sabrina made his hands clammy and his stomach ache. Carrie was more like a best friend's adorable little sister. Balling his fist, he pounded it on the desk. *But, God, I don't want to think of Sabrina like this. She's completely wrong for me, and she doesn't love You.*

He thought of the three words she'd uttered when she cried on his chest, *"Not her, too."* What had she meant by that? The pitiful words and pain-filled expression had eaten at him for two days. Had she miscarried a child?

He'd suspected something when she'd stormed out of his office at the pregnancy center the first time he'd met her. But since then he'd talked with Mallory several times. She'd asked him to pray for Sabrina but never hinted that her sister had had an abortion or miscarriage. He knew so little about Sabrina, but there were a few things very evident. She loved her sister and would do anything for her. And she fought God with every ounce of her being. But why?

His heart beat against his chest. He couldn't avoid her. Deep inside, he didn't even want to. Despite his feelings for Sabrina, he needed to be a good counselor to Mallory. A godly encouragement. Pulling his phone from his pocket, he searched his address book for Mallory's number. She picked up on the first ring. "Hi, Mallory. It's Brent. How are you?"

"I'm great." She sounded happy, well rested. "No troubles at all today."

He knew that meant she hadn't experienced any more spotting.

"Would you like me to bring you and your sister some dinner?"

"Mmm, yes. Sabrina cooked, but it didn't work so well for her," said Mallory.

He bit back a chuckle when he heard Sabrina's voice in the background. "I heard that."

Mallory continued, "Actually, Sabrina is a terrific cook. I don't know what happened with her concoction tonight. But you know what I'm in the mood for?"

"What?" he asked.

Again he heard Sabrina's voice in the background. "Who are you talking to?"

"Sushi. But Sabrina hates Asian food," said Mallory.

"Who are you talking to?" Sabrina asked again. This time her voice sounded closer.

"But she loves burgers." A struggle sounded over the line; then Mallory said in a muffled tone, "Come quick before she takes my phone and tries to tell you we can fend for ourselves."

The call ended, and Brent laughed outright. He would ignore any calls from Mallory's number, because he knew the girl was right. Sabrina would try to talk him out of bringing them something to eat. The woman needed to learn to let others help out every once in a while. She didn't have to do everything for herself.

He thought of his two-year-old niece who often furrowed her brow and puckered up her lips whenever he tried to help her with her shoes. *"I do it myself!"* Brooke would yank the shoes from his grip, plop down on the floor, and fight with her shoes. *Sabrina's as bad as Brooke.*

He locked up the pantry and stopped by his favorite Chinese restaurant. After picking up several kinds of sushi for Mallory, he drove to the other side of town to get burgers and fries from the place where he'd shared dinner with Sabrina. She'd said she really liked their burgers.

As he drove to their house, he debated if he should ask to eat with them or just take his dinner out of the bag, go home, and eat by himself. Probably just dropping off their food would be better. Butterflies fluttered in his stomach as he pulled into the driveway. He scooped up the bags and walked to the front door then realized he'd forgotten to take his dinner out of the bag. He rolled his eyes at himself. He was a grown man with a job, a mortgage, and a car payment, and he was still getting flustered over a woman.

He turned to put his food back in the car when the front door opened. Mallory grabbed him in a bear hug. "The cavalry has arrived." She grabbed the bag from the Chinese restaurant from his grasp. "I've been dying for sushi."

She motioned him inside. "Come on in. Did you bring food for yourself? If not, I'll share. A little."

Brent chuckled. "I brought my own. I got Sabrina a burger and fries, like you said."

Mallory huffed. "She's hiding in the kitchen. She can't believe I let you get our dinner." She pointed to the back of the house. "Back there. She'll be nicer to you than to me. I'm going back to the couch."

Brent walked in the direction she'd pointed. Sabrina's house was decorated just as he would have expected. Contemporary. Flashy—in bright reds and deep purples. And everything was spotless. It looked as if no one lived here.

Passing through a door, he spied Sabrina leaning against the kitchen sink, her arms crossed in front of her chest. "I'm sorry Mallory asked you to bring us dinner."

"I offered."

"I forgot," Mallory yelled from the living room. "Thanks for the sushi, Brent."

Sabrina shook her head and pursed her lips. Brent grinned. "No problem, Mallory," he yelled back. He lifted the burger bag up higher. "If I remember right, you enjoyed their burgers."

"I did." She squinted. "But I bet you didn't know I eat my burger with ketchup and mustard and no mayo."

He placed the bag on the small table, lifted out the hamburgers and fries then pulled out condiment packets. "Which is why I asked them not to put the condiments on the burger. To simply put them in the bag."

Sabrina lifted her brows and nodded. "You're good. You must be a pro at wining and dining women."

Brent shook his head. "No. I was just raised by a mother

and with two sisters. Dad and I learned there is no pleasing a woman when it comes to dressing her food."

Sabrina laughed a full-bellied sound that filled him with pleasure. Again, she wasn't wearing makeup. He marveled at her natural beauty and wondered why she hid herself behind so much paint. She motioned for him to have a seat. "What would you like to drink? Regular or diet or water?"

He sat in front of the loaded-with-everything burger he'd ordered for himself. "Regular."

She placed a canned drink in front of him. He popped the lid and waited for her to sit across from him. "Do you mind if I pray?"

The words slipped out before he'd had time to think about how Sabrina might feel about the question. It was her home, and her animosity toward God was obvious.

She huffed. "Knock yourself out. Everybody else who comes through my door these days sure does."

Sabrina remained still as Brent spoke his prayer over the food. Her chest tightened when he thanked God that Mallory and the baby were fine. She, too, was grateful, so relieved that both were safe. Now that Mallory stayed with her, Sabrina could protect her and the unborn child.

She would have never imagined when Mallory called her to the college apartment, the night they'd learned Mallory was pregnant, that Sabrina would have become so emotionally connected to the child so quickly. She longed to see him or her, to see if the baby shared Mallory's hair color or the almond shape of her eyes.

Grateful her parents' social status forced them to keep Mallory on their insurance plan, Sabrina would have no problem making sure her sister received the best medical care throughout the pregnancy. It pained her that neither her mom nor her dad had contacted Sabrina or Mallory since they'd shared the news of their upcoming grandchild. Sabrina had even called to tell them Mallory was in the hospital. The phone had gone straight to voice mail, and no return call was made.

Sabrina gritted her teeth and waited for Brent to finish. Weren't prayers before meals supposed to be a quick, "thanks for the food" kind of thing? The guy rambled through a list of blessings and petitions that seemed to take forever.

He muttered an amen then looked up at her. Sabrina hadn't realized how blue his eyes were. They were a deep color that reminded her of the ocean, not toward the shore but a few miles out where its depth is indistinguishable to the naked eye. They glistened contentment and peace in a way she'd never known but wanted to.

"You have beautiful eyes." The words slipped through her lips with an air of vulnerability and longing. Realizing she'd let down her guard, she blinked and sat up taller in the chair. Determined to stay in control, she refused to shift her gaze from his.

He offered a slow grin, and she forced herself not to think about how he seemed to get more handsome each time she saw him. "I could say the same to you. Yours look like drops of dark chocolate."

Sabrina nodded. Many men had complimented her eyes, among other things, but Brent's tone was different. His words didn't come with a wink or a flirtatious hope for more than she was willing to share. He picked up his hamburger and took a bite. She nibbled on a french fry but continued to study him. He wasn't gorgeous in a *GQ* model kind of way, but he was nice looking. A bit tall. Maybe a tad too thin. But he had a strong chin, straight white teeth, and an adorable head of wavy hair. And his eyes were beguiling. How hadn't she noticed that before?

He swallowed his bite of food then took a drink. "It seems every time I talk with you it's after some sort of emergency or calamity."

Sabrina chuckled. "Very true."

He shrugged. "Since nothing bad is happening today, how about some small talk?"

She nodded. "Okay."

"So tell me a bit about yourself."

"I work for a coffee shop chain. Do the books and some managing for several places. How 'bout you? You work full-time at the pregnancy center?"

"I do. I'm also a volunteer director for our local food pantry."

"That's great." Sabrina felt unease rising inside her. She'd never had trouble talking with a man before. If they acted in a way she didn't like, she left. No games played and no emotional connections. It was easier that way. A girl didn't get hurt.

But there was something about Brent. He just seemed so...she couldn't quite put her finger on it. Genuine, maybe? He didn't seem to *want* anything from her. He was too easy to talk with. Too nice. She wasn't used to that.

Josif had been the last man who hadn't pressured her or acted as if he had ulterior motives, be it a pretty woman on his arm for the world to see or the hope of other things. Josif was wrapped up in his work, and she had liked that. They were both driven to be at the top of their careers. But he wasn't who she thought he was. And when his future wife came along, he apparently figured that Sabrina wasn't who he wanted, either. She'd wasted three years on that relationship.

"So, you got a boyfriend?"

Sabrina almost laughed aloud at his question. Was he reading her thoughts? Instead, she shook her head. "No."

She pointed to their meal. "Don't you remember the last time we ate this together that I'd had a bit of a letdown from a computer date?"

He nodded. "That's right." He pointed to himself. "I don't have a girlfriend, either."

She cocked her head. "Why not? You seem like a nice guy."

He chuckled and lifted his chin. "I am a nice guy, and I want one. A girlfriend, I mean. Just waiting for God to bring the right woman into my life."

"I believe you told me that at the hamburger joint."

"That's right. Sorry 'bout that."

"It's okay." She studied him again. He still wasn't flirting. He acted as if she were a friend. "I thought I had met the man I'd marry. We dated for three years, but then Josif met Mirela and…"

Brent furrowed his brows and leaned forward. "Did you just say Josif and Mirela?"

"Yes?"

"What's their last name?"

"Sesely."

He smacked the top of the table, and she blinked and sat back. "You are kidding me, right?"

Sabrina shook her head.

"I know them." He leaned back his head and laughed. "Would you like to know how I know them?"

Sabrina shrugged, though she was a bit apprehensive. "Sure."

Josif's family most likely did not hold her in the highest regard. She couldn't deny she'd behaved badly to Mirela after she and Josif broke up. She didn't really mourn Josif as she should have if she'd truly been in love with him, but she was mad at the rejection. *She* broke up with guys. They did not break up with her.

Brent dropped his napkin onto the table, a grin still spreading his lips. "Have you ever met Mirela's sister, Ivy?"

She remembered visiting the sisters' church and then going to their house for lunch. She was a pretty blond who could have been a knockout if she'd just worn a little makeup and gotten a newer hairstyle. "Once."

"I liked her for a while. Tried to get her to go out. Her mom liked me, too. But she fell for a contractor with a ready-made family." He laughed again.

Somehow, she didn't find it quite as amusing as he did. It didn't seem like that big of a deal. So they both knew the family. Who cares? What? Was Brent still pining over Mirela's sister?

"Would you like to know how they're all doing?"

Not really. She couldn't say that aloud. It would be rude. "Sure."

"Mirela and Josif adopted Benny and Bella."

She remembered those kids. Mirela babysat them. She wasn't surprised that Josif and Mirela would adopt them. Probably good for the kids. Their mom seemed a little messed up.

"They've got a child of their own as well. A little girl."

Sabrina wasn't surprised. Josif had been all about business when they were together, but when Mirela came along he turned all churchy. Decided he wanted to settle down and have a bunch of kids.

"Ivy's pregnant. Not even married a year and she and Carter will have their fourth child. Of course, the first three were with his wife who'd passed away."

Sabrina nodded. By the mirth in his expression, she could tell Ivy's growing family didn't upset him. At least he wasn't pining after the girl.

"That's quite a coincidence, huh?" he said.

"What?"

He laughed. "That you and Josif didn't work out, but he ended up with Mirela. And that Ivy and I didn't work out, but she ended up with Carter. That leaves me and you."

She stared at him as his neck and cheeks began to turn pink. *He must have realized what he said. Well, good. Because I don't find this conversation funny.*

Chapter 7

I am a buffoon. A big, overgrown, skinny idiot. Though a week had passed, every time he thought of the conversation he'd had with Sabrina at her house he wanted to wring his own neck. He'd been so nervous. The woman was beautiful. Too much so. She was without a physical flaw. Sitting with her at the table alone, he'd been a barrel of nerves. As a result, he spent most of the evening talking about her ex and his wannabe ex.

He smacked his hand against his forehead and mumbled, "What was I thinking?"

"I don't know because that was not a good shot." Will grabbed the basketball after it bounced off the rim and launched it back in the air. "But that one is."

The ball swished through the net, and Will flipped his wrist. "All in the wrist, man."

Brent scooped the ball from beneath the net, dribbled out to the three point line then drove in and dunked. "But I betcha can't do that."

Will scoffed. "Dude, I'm five-eight. I've never been able to do that."

Brent laughed, as he bent down and rubbed his right knee. Landing didn't feel like it did ten years ago.

Will tossed the ball to Brent. "You still coming over for dinner?"

"Planning on it."

"Just so you know, we'll be having company."

Brent raised one eyebrow. "What does that mean?"

Will sighed. "I'm not supposed to tell you, but I told Tab it's not fair to just spring stuff on people."

"Tell me what?"

"Carrie's going to be there."

Brent tucked the ball under his arm. "Why? The girl stood me up."

Will walked off the basketball court. He picked up a washcloth and wiped his face. "She did not stand you up. She got sick."

Brent raised his hands in surrender. "All I know is every time I ask the girl to go anywhere or do anything she's got other plans or she gets sick."

"Give the girl a break. She really likes you."

Brent released a long breath. She certainly had an odd way of showing it. Her nerves reminded him of dating in middle school. And he had never enjoyed those years. They were filled with awkwardness and frustration. He took a drink of his water. However, seeing Carrie might get his mind off Sabrina.

"I was going to have you help me put up the Christmas lights, too."

"What? It's the second week of November. Is that why Jason skipped out on us today? He knew you needed help?"

Will laughed. "I did mention it at work. Maybe that caused his headache." He sobered. "Come on, man. It's so much easier for you, and the weather's nice. Besides, I'll help you put up your lights."

"I don't have Christmas lights for the outside of my house."

"Well, then it will be super easy."

Brent shook his head and chuckled. "What time?"

"Go home and shower then come on over. We'll do the Christmas stuff first."

"Okay." Brent gathered his things and headed out of the gym. Once home, he showered and put on his favorite University of Tennessee sweatshirt. If he weren't going to be climbing on Will's roof, he would wear something nicer. But for all he knew, Carrie wouldn't show anyway.

Once he made it to Will's house, his friend barely let him get out of the car before he had him standing on a ladder and hanging icicles from his roof. Will set out the lighted reindeer while Brent risked his neck.

Will's youngest daughter, three-year-old Maddy, pushed through the front door. She stood on the sidewalk, clapping. "Pwetty lights, Bwentie."

Brent looked down at the blond cherub and knew he'd put lights all over the roof if she wanted him to. The ten-year-old came outside and grabbed her sister's hand. "Mom wants to know if y'all want a drink."

"Yes, please," said Brent.

"Same as always?" said Molly.

"Yep."

"Me, too," said Will. "Thanks, sweetie."

Brent turned back to the lights. He was almost done. Just one more strand to hook together then he could call it quits. Thankfully, his friend had a modest-sized house. A car pulled into the driveway and Carrie stepped out. She'd gotten her hair cut. It was styled straight and barely touched her shoulders. It looked nice. Made her look a little more grown-up.

"Hey, guys," she said.

"Hi, Carrie." Brent watched as she went inside the house. He hoped she'd be herself in front of him today.

He finished the last strand as Molly came outside with his soft drink. After making his way down the ladder, he took a long drink. "You almost done?"

"Yep. Just gotta attach the sled to the reindeer."

Brent grinned at his friend's yard. It was filled with various Christmas decorations from angels to reindeer to a nativity to a Santa and his sleigh. A few more years of after-Christmas-sale-buying and his house would rival Chevy Chase's in the movie *National Lampoon's Christmas Vacation.*

With the outside finished, they walked into the house. Brent inhaled the spicy Mexican aroma. No one made tacos and burritos like Tab.

"Hope the food's ready. We're starving," said Will.

"It smells delicious," added Brent. He tugged on Maddy's single braid. The child squealed then jumped around and landed a karate chop into his leg. Brent sparred with her until he had to lift his hands in defeat.

"It's ready. Clean up and have a seat," Tab said.

Brent hadn't seen Carrie since she'd come in the house. By the time he sat down, everyone was there except her. *If she's gotten sick or run out of here or whatever, I'm calling it quits on trying to get to know this girl. God, You'll have to show me someone else. But keep my mind off Sabrina. Please.*

He gritted his teeth just thinking her name. He'd done well for most of the day. Tried not to think about the tall brunette. Wouldn't do him any good even if he wanted to, she inevitably thought he was crazy.

Carrie walked into the room and sat across from him. She averted her gaze, and then Will offered a blessing over the food. The table came to life with all of them passing plates of food and chattering about what had happened that day. But Carrie remained quiet.

Brent bit back a growl. This wasn't going to work. He needed a woman who would at least be able to look at him through dinner. They finished the meal, and Brent helped Will clear the table while Tab cleaned up Maddy and Carrie helped Molly do something. He had no idea what the woman was doing. Avoiding him, for one.

"This isn't going to work," Brent whispered to Will.

Will furrowed his brow. "She is really shy in front of you. Normally she's a lot of fun."

"Great. So I'm a killjoy."

Will shrugged. "Guess so."

Brent scowled, and Will laughed.

"Hey guys, we thought we'd go bowling," Tab yelled from the other room.

Will bristled. "Now honey, what are we going to do with the girls? You know we have to make plans—"

"Just get in here," she yelled again.

Brent followed Will into the living area. Tab and Carrie had moved the furniture to allow a large space in front of the television. Will widened his eyes when he saw Tab holding up two remote controls. "When did we get a Wii?"

"It's Carrie's. She thought it would be fun to show you boys how to bowl."

Carrie grinned, and Brent saw a glint of mischief in her eyes. It was the same look he'd seen the day in the food pantry when she'd teased him. He loved to bowl. And he was especially good on the Wii. She may be in for more than she'd bargained for.

"You wanna play?" Carrie asked him.

"You wanna lose?"

Carrie grinned and motioned for Tab to hand them the controllers. The game started. She was better than he thought, bowling three strikes in a row to his two spares and one strike. She nudged his arm with her elbow. "You're going to have to up your game."

Brent grinned. He loved a sports challenge, even if they were technically playing a video game. The score drew closer when she bowled a few spares and he started hitting strikes. They were down to the last roll. It was his turn. He only needed to hit three pins to win the game. He pulled back his hand to let the ball loose, and Carrie jumped on his back. He released early and hit the gutter.

He twirled her around. "Hey! No fair."

Carrie squealed, and Maddy joined her by wrapping her body around his leg. "Tackle, Bwent," she hollered.

In the blink of an eye, Molly grabbed his arm and pulled until he found himself falling to the ground. Molly hopped on top of one leg, and Maddy grabbed the other one. Carrie pinned down both his arms and stuck out her tongue. "I won."

He didn't know who this new Carrie was, but she was a lot of fun. Someone he definitely wanted to get to know better.

Sabrina pushed the grocery cart toward the checkout lane. She turned toward Mallory. "You're sure we got everything?"

Mallory looked at the list. "Everything's checked off."

Sabrina bit her bottom lip. She leaned over the cart and rummaged through the food items. Celery sticks. A package of stuffing. Two pie crusts. Whipped topping. Pumpkin pie filling. "It seems like we're missing something."

"Sabrina, we've checked the list twice."

"Maybe I forgot to write it down."

Mallory grabbed her hand. "What is *it*?"

"I don't know." Releasing a sigh of frustration, Sabrina pushed the cart into the lane and started putting items on the conveyor belt. They hadn't seen their parents since the day Mallory told them about the baby. The invitation to come for Thanksgiving dinner the next week had come as a surprise. It shouldn't have. It should be expected that they'd spend the holiday with their parents.

"It's going to be okay." Mallory put her hand on Sabrina's shoulder. "God's got this."

Sabrina rolled her eyes. That made her feel so much better. Mallory may believe in her unseen God, but Sabrina lived in the real world—a place where people made their own choices and reached their own goals through intelligence and hard work; a world where people didn't just forgive and forget the things that angered them. Especially people like her parents.

She bit her bottom lip again. And yet, the change in her sister was undeniable. She'd handled the unplanned pregnancy and miscarriage scare with a peace Sabrina had never seen in her sister. Mallory had even kept up with her schoolwork and was making all As, something she'd never done in high school.

Once she'd finished emptying the groceries from the cart, Sabrina looked at the cashier. She cringed at the girl who was probably a year or two younger than Mallory. Her shirt was tight around her fully pregnant midsection. Though she appeared clean enough, the girl sported small diamond nose and lip rings, and her long hair was dyed black with a blond streak down the right side.

"When's your baby due?" asked Mallory.

Sabrina glared at her sister. They had no reason to make small talk with the juvenile delinquent. What were the girl's parents thinking, allowing her to look like that? She shook her head when she realized her thoughts sounded very much like what her own mom would say.

"December 25th," the girl answered.

Mallory clapped. "How fun!"

"Yeah. It's a terrific Christmas present."

The girl's deadpan tone jerked at Sabrina's heart. What if the girl's parents weren't involved in her life? Sabrina didn't look like the cashier, but she would have been in a world of financial trouble if she had tried to keep the baby when she was nineteen. Not that she had the option.

"I'm due May 30th." Mallory patted her belly. "Not showing yet, though."

The girl nodded then told Sabrina the total. She pulled out her debit card and swiped it through the machine. The girl probably hadn't finished high school. Sabrina wondered if she was trying to. Maybe she had a boyfriend who was going to help with the baby. Sabrina was concerned about how her sister would handle the challenges of raising a baby, but Mallory would have Sabrina's help. And Mallory was receiving guidance from the pregnancy center. Who was helping this young girl? Putting the debit card back in her wallet, Sabrina spied one of Brent's cards in the pocket of her purse. Her face warmed as she pulled it out and handed it to the girl. "You may not need this, but I know the center can help you with questions, concerns, or financial resources."

Mallory's eyebrows lifted with the full smile that took over her expression. "Yeah. They're great. They've been helping me with my pregnancy."

A flicker of hope spread across the girl's features when she took the card. Her expression shifted back to disinterest and apathy. "Thanks."

Sabrina pushed the cart out of the lane and toward the

exit. Mallory walked beside her. Sabrina could feel the silly grin plastered across her sister's face. She didn't look at her. "What?"

"You know what."

"No. I don't."

Mallory touched her hand. "You have a good heart."

Sabrina rolled her eyes. "Please. I saw the business card when I went to put my debit card back in my wallet, so I gave it to her. No big deal."

"I think God's softening your heart."

Sabrina popped open the trunk. She had no intention of arguing with her sister over God. The center had been good for Mallory. They could probably help the girl. That was all there was to it. Besides, she didn't want to spend her life judging everyone as her parents had always done. That didn't mean she thought one way or the other about God.

She thought of Brent's prayer the night he'd brought the hamburgers and sushi. His sincerity had haunted her. He'd babbled on about her ex and his wife and the girl he'd wanted to date, which kind of got on her nerves. But she'd enjoyed the way he talked to her, like she was a person he wanted to get to know, not a goal or a trophy.

It seemed like forever since she'd seen him. Mallory had gone to the center several times since that night to see Vanessa or talk with Brent or one of the other ladies. Sabrina wondered how he was doing.

"I didn't tell you. I met up with the baby's father yesterday."

Sabrina furrowed her brow and looked at her sister. "What?"

Mallory pointed to her belly. "I found out the guy's name and tracked him down on campus."

Sabrina shook her head. "Why?"

"I just thought it was only fair. Besides he had to know. He'd have to sign away his rights anyway."

Sabrina bit her bottom lip. Actually, she hadn't thought much about the baby's father. It had been a one-night stand. The guy probably freaked out and said some unkind things to her sister. Sabrina's stomach twisted. The guy had better have been nice. "What did he say?"

"It was so weird." Mallory opened the passenger door and placed one arm on the roof. "He'd felt bad about that night. Said it wasn't like him. You'll never believe this."

"What?"

"The guy had been wanting to apologize to me. He knew who I was. Had even followed me to class on a couple of occasions."

"Why? Is he some kind of stalker? Did he force himself?"

Mallory shook her head. "No. He just felt bad. Said he should have never been there to begin with. That he'd never done anything like that. Just got caught up in the first few weeks of college. Just like me. You know why he felt bad?"

"Why?"

" 'Cause he's a Christian."

Mallory slipped inside the car. Sabrina exhaled a long breath. She stared out past the shopping center and toward the Smoky Mountains. Even with most of the leaves gone, the land was pure beauty. Serenity.

She'd had just about all she could take of this Christianity stuff. It had ruined her relationship with Josif and changed her sister. What kind of Christian guy would go to a party, get drunk, and have sex with a college girl? She knew all kinds of guys who would do it, but Christians were supposed to be different. A bumper sticker she'd read a few weeks ago that stated Christians weren't perfect, just saved, slipped through her mind. *Well, that boy most defi-nitely hadn't been perfect.*

She got into the car. "So what does that mean?"

"He wants to help. In fact, he wants to be a part of the baby's life. I want you to meet him."

Sabrina gripped the steering wheel. She'd agreed to help her sister—wanted to do it—but she had no desire to deal with a guy her sister barely knew. She wanted it to be her and Mallory taking care of the baby. Not some random guy. Even if he was the biological father.

Chapter 8

Brent shut off his office computer. He was looking forward to the next few days of Thanksgiving celebration. At his parents' house, he'd eat until he was sick; then he and his dad and brothers-in-law would watch his six nephews and nieces while his mother and sisters shopped from before sunup until well past sundown on Black Friday.

He'd considered asking Carrie to his family's Thanksgiving. They'd gone out once since dinner at Will and Tab's and had seen each other several times at the food pantry. He liked her. She was a nice girl. But something stopped him from inviting her. He didn't feel quite ready to start a relationship with her.

A knock sounded on his door. He looked at his clock, knowing he should have left fifteen minutes ago. Part of him wanted to help anyone in need. The other part was ready to go home and take a break. Lifting up a quick prayer for wisdom and patience, he said, "Come on in."

He was surprised when the tall, dark-haired beauty who captured his thoughts more times than she ought walked inside. He nodded. "Hello, Sabrina."

She stood across from his desk, wringing her hands and chewing on her bottom lip. Frustration etched her brow. "Do you have a minute?"

"Sure." He motioned for her to take a seat, and he sat as well. Concern niggled at him, and he hoped all was well. Mallory had been in the office just today. Everything seemed fine. She'd even brought the baby's father with her. Realization hit him. That was probably what was wrong.

"Have you met Jacob?"

He nodded. Just as he'd guessed. The father of Mallory's baby had been quite a surprise to him. The guy was clean cut, super nice, the oldest son in a middle-class family of three boys, made good grades, had a true desire to teach high school and coach wrestling. And he was a Christian. A guy who'd felt deep conviction about his choice that night. He was not a typical one-night stand.

"What do you think about him?"

Brent clasped his hands. He had to tread carefully here. He couldn't break any patient/client confidentiality, but he'd prayed for Sabrina more often than he'd ever prayed for anyone. He didn't want to simply turn her away, either. *As long as I keep the focus off Jacob and on God. Help me, Lord.*

"He seems like a nice young man."

Sabrina squinted. "I know. He's great. Wonderful. I actually really like him."

Brent frowned. He could only guess where she was going with this. "Okay."

"He says he's a Christian."

"Okay."

Sabrina scooted to the edge of the chair. She placed her

arms on his desk and lifted her palms up. "Mallory wasn't a Christian yet when it happened. She got caught up in"— she lifted her hands and made quotation gestures—"sin, but she hadn't made any commitments to God until after she was already pregnant. So, if he was already a Christian, why would he get drunk and sleep with my sister?"

Brent swallowed. *God, help me. Give me the right words to say.* "Sabrina, Christians still make mistakes."

She cocked her head. "That seems like an awfully big mistake. So does that mean Christians can just go out and do anything they want? Cheat? Steal? Kill? And it's just that they made a mistake?"

"No. Not at all."

"It sounds like it. So, if I accept Christ, I can live however I want and still go to heaven?"

"No, Sabrina." Brent reached out and touched her hand. Electricity shot through him and he pulled away, afraid she could feel the spark running through his fingertips. He blinked. He shouldn't respond to the softness of her skin in such a way. Especially when he liked Carrie. Shaking the thoughts away, he cleared his throat. "Have you ever heard of Paul from the Bible?"

Sabrina shrugged. "Probably. I've been to church tons of times. I just…"

Brent didn't wait for her to try to finish. "He was a man who had been born with everything, according to the standards of Bible times. He was a Roman, a Pharisee, which was kind of like a head religious leader. He even persecuted the Christians. Then Jesus met him on the Damascus Road, and he received Christ into his heart."

Sabrina shrugged. "So he changed, right? Mallory has changed. I see the difference in her."

"Yes, but even after Jesus saved him, he wrote that he constantly struggled with the flesh"—he pointed to his heart—"the sin that dwells in all of us. He talked about how he wanted to do the right thing and yet he fought doing the right thing. That there was a constant battle over doing God's will and his own will."

Sabrina chewed her bottom lip as she stared at the wall beside her. He knew she contemplated his words, and he prayed God would open her heart, that she would receive Him as Lord. She gazed up at him, and Brent found himself longing to take her in his arms, to assure her that if she would only accept Christ that He would help her understand. Things wouldn't always be easy, but she would always be safe in His hands.

"If I'm going to fight myself all the time over good and bad, why would I want to be a Christian?"

"Because salvation leads to eternal life in heaven. It also leads to peace here on earth, when we follow God's will."

Sabrina huffed. "Mallory is not in the midst of peace right now. She's nineteen and getting ready to have a baby. And Jacob is trying to get a full-time job to help cover the baby's expenses. Doesn't sound like a life of peace to me."

"Being a Christian doesn't mean life is easy. We still face hardships, whether it's because of sin or simply because we're living in a world that isn't perfect."

Sabrina stared past him again. He knew her brain churned through his words. She looked gorgeous in dark blue jeans and a red jacket. The silky gray shirt underneath sparkled with small sequins. Her dark hair was piled up on the top of her head with only a few strands falling along her cheeks. Though he wasn't a fan of the makeup and boisterous, silver, dangling earrings, they fit Sabrina. And the bright red lipstick on her lips drew him in a way he couldn't deny.

Forcing himself to look away from her, he sat up straighter in his chair. He shouldn't think of her that way.

If she became a Christian, maybe things could be different. He pushed away the thought. If he were going to plan for that, then he didn't need to date Carrie. But he wanted to date Carrie. She was fun, and he wanted to keep his mind off Sabrina.

Ugh. God, I'm every bit as bad as Paul, fighting myself over what I should and shouldn't want.

"And yet, you haven't asked Me."

The Spirit's nudging caught him by surprise. What was there to ask? Sabrina wasn't a child of God. Carrie was. Carrie was the obvious better choice.

Maybe it's not about needing to make a choice right now. Maybe I'm not supposed to be dating at all.

He pushed the thought aside. He would be twenty-nine in only a few months. He'd wanted to be married longer than any of his friends, and he was the last bachelor. It was his turn, and he was tired of waiting. Carrie was a terrific woman. Any guy would be lucky to have her.

Sabrina stood, and Brent shook off his inner battle. He looked up at her, and a knot formed in his throat. She was entirely too beautiful.

"I'm going to have to think about all this."

She turned, and Brent hopped out of his seat. "Wait, Sabrina?" She turned toward him again. "Maybe I could send you some scriptures for you to look up. I could text them to you."

She nodded. "That's fine." She smiled, even though he could tell it was forced. "Enjoy your Thanksgiving."

"You, too."

She huffed. "I'll try."

Mallory had told him they were going to their parents' for Thanksgiving. She'd asked him to pray for the visit, which would most likely be strained at best. After Sabrina shut the door behind her, Brent flopped back into his chair.

His inner turmoil over Sabrina exhausted him. Before he sent her the scriptures, he'd need to look over them himself.

Sabrina lifted the pumpkin pies out of the oven. They smelled delicious. She placed them on the cooling rack then wiped her hands on a towel. She'd spent a good portion of the day googling the scriptures Brent had texted to her. She'd heard them all in the various churches she'd attended over the years. Jesus was the only way to salvation. She had to repent of her sins. Accept Him into her heart. She'd had to read the one written by Paul about doing what you don't want to do and not doing what you want to do at least ten times before she finally understood what he was saying. But the scriptures didn't help her. All of them essentially said that she'd have to trust God with her life. All of it. And that simply wasn't going to happen.

She took out the ingredients to make the stuffing. After rinsing off the celery, she cut the spears into small pieces. She took off a piece and chomped into it. She'd skipped lunch to save room for dinner, and she was starving. Mallory should be home soon. She wondered how her day had gone.

Jacob invited her to Thanksgiving with his family. Sabrina would have never agreed, but Mallory said, "They'll have to get to know me sometime. I'm having their grandbaby."

Sabrina wrinkled her nose. She didn't want to think about people she'd never met before fawning over Mallory's baby. Even if she did like Jacob. Even if having a little bit of help would be nice. Sabrina and Mallory certainly wouldn't get any from their parents.

Measuring the water, she poured it in the pot and then put it on the stove to heat. She wondered how her parents would act today. Probably they'd pretend everything was as it had always been. Or they'd throw a fit and insist on an abortion. *If they even mention it, I'm grabbing Mallory by the hand, and we are out of there.*

She didn't want to think about it. Besides, they'd find out soon enough. Looking at the clock on the microwave, she realized they'd have to leave in less than half an hour. Mallory should have been home by now. She walked into the living area and peeked out the front window. Jacob and Mallory stood in front of his car. He held her hands in his. Sabrina's heart tightened when he leaned down and kissed her cheek.

Jealousy niggled at her gut, and Sabrina walked away from the window. She must be getting soft. A month or two ago she'd have grumbled over the affection she saw growing between Mallory and Jacob. Now, she wished she could experience it.

Brent popped into her mind. She could imagine him offering a chaste kiss on the cheek. He was nothing like the men she normally dated. Not driven by his career. Not covered in muscles. Not pushy or arrogant. The last two qualities she had to admit she especially liked.

Pushing the thought away, she walked back into the kitchen and finished making the stuffing. She spooned it into a serving bowl then wrapped the stuffing and pies with cellophane. Mallory still hadn't come inside. *What in the world could they be doing out there?*

She made her way into the bedroom and slipped on her shoes. Mallory opened the door before Sabrina had to go get her. "I'm back," her sister yelled.

"Don't take off your shoes. Come grab the stuffing. We've got to go."

"'Kay." Mallory practically floated into the kitchen. She scooped the stuffing off the counter, a smile spreading her lips.

Sabrina bit back a laugh. "Have a good time?"

Mallory's eyes glistened. "I'll tell you about it in the car."

Sabrina nodded, and they walked outside, put the dishes in the backseat, and got in the car. Once in their seats and buckled up, Sabrina started the car and pulled out of the driveway. "Okay. Spill it."

"They're wonderful," Mallory gushed. "His little brothers were adorable, eight-year-old twins, and his parents were so sweet. They were happy to meet me. After we ate, they sat us down and talked to us about how God can take a difficult situation and use it for good. His dad actually read all of chapter eight of Romans to us."

Sabrina made a mental note to look up that scripture when she got home.

"They told us God didn't like our sin, but that with our repentance, God would make good of the situation. And I believe He will."

Sabrina tossed her sister's words around in her mind. They sounded so much like what Brent had said to her. But the baby wasn't here yet, and though Sabrina had limited experience with a newborn, she felt confident the baby would make things more difficult than either of them expected.

"Then Jacob told me he wants us to try to get to know each other better. He wants me to be his girlfriend."

Her voice caught, and Sabrina peeked at her sister. Her neck and cheeks turned crimson, and again Sabrina felt the niggling of jealousy. Pulling into her parents' driveway, her stomach plummeted. She had a feeling the rest of the evening wouldn't go as kindly.

"Don't stress, Sabrina."

She looked at her baby sister who had matured so much

in the last few months. Sabrina wished for the peace Mallory exuded. "You're right. If they're ugly, we'll leave."

Mallory clicked her tongue. "Have a little faith."

Easier said than done. Sabrina bit back the retort as she parked the car. They grabbed the dishes and made their way into the house.

"Girls, I'm so glad you're here." Her mother opened her arms and wrapped one around each of them. "It's been too long."

And whose fault is that? Again, she bit back her reply. Her mother would behave just as expected, as if nothing had happened and nothing had changed.

"So, how are classes, Mallory?" asked their dad.

"As long as my finals go well, I'll make all As."

"Really?"

Sabrina sighed at the surprised tone in her father's voice. Mallory was doing better than she had in high school, but if her parents had taken the time to check on her, they would have known that.

"How's the coffee business?"

He turned his attention to Sabrina, and she plastered a forced smile on her lips. "Everything is great."

"Here, let's get these dishes on the table," said their mom. "Sabrina, the pies look delicious."

Sabrina followed her mother into the dining area. The table was set for four with pristine china. Turkey, mashed potatoes, gravy, green bean, corn, and sweet potato casseroles, fruit salad, deviled eggs, and cranberry sauce covered the table. As frustrating as her mother could be, Sabrina could not deny she was a superb cook. She put down the stuffing. "Mom, it looks and smells so good."

"Thank you, dear."

Sabrina chewed the inside of her lip. With just the two of them in here, maybe she could see if her mom had come around a bit regarding Mallory's pregnancy. She wrung her hands together. "Mom, Mallory has a doctor's appointment in two weeks."

Her mother lifted her eyebrows. "Really? What for?"

"It's a monthly appointment. Maybe you'd like to come with us?"

Her mother squinted and pursed her lips. "We will not discuss it. As far as I'm concerned, *it* doesn't exist."

Sabrina's stomach churned at her mother's exaggeration at the word *it*. So that was how they would handle the pregnancy. Pretend it never happened. "What are you going to do when *it* is born?"

Her mother lifted her finger and shook her head. "Not another word."

Sabrina glared at her mother as Mallory and her father walked into the room. Mallory sat in her usual seat and continued to talk about her psychology class while their father sat in the chair beside her. He looked up at Sabrina and patted the chair on the opposite side. "Sit down. I can't wait to sample each dish."

Sabrina wanted to grab Mallory's hand and walk out. She hated the shallowness of their parents, the way they could pretend nothing was wrong when they hadn't even checked on their daughter when she'd been in the hospital. *God, I don't want to be like them.*

The silent prayer caught her off guard, and she furrowed her brow. Since when did she share her frustrations with God? She rubbed her temple with her right hand. She was tired. Tired of games. Tired of trying to make sense of things.

She heard her sister chattering with their parents, unable to understand how Mallory could be so kind to them. She didn't even want to be in the same house as them. She speared pieces of turkey and placed them on her plate.

For her sister's sake, she would suffer through this meal. If she had her way, this would be the last time they came.

"Do you mind if I say a quick prayer?" asked Mallory.

Sabrina lifted her eyebrows and looked from her mother to her father. Her dad shrugged and bowed his head. Sabrina followed. She couldn't believe Mallory had gotten them to agree to pray.

Chapter 9

Brent followed his dad into the kitchen. "Why don't you let me make breakfast this year?"

His dad bristled. "I have made pancakes for my grandchildren every Black Friday since Allie was born. I think I can handle this."

"I know, Dad. I'm just worried about your knee."

His dad pulled a plastic bowl from the cabinet then grabbed a spatula from the counter. He nodded toward the living room. "I reckon you better go check on the young'uns and get on out of here."

"Let him be." Laura's husband, Nick, patted his shoulder. "No need to cause a ruckus." Nick grabbed his coat off the rack.

"Where are you going?"

"To help Matt put up the Christmas lights."

Brent blew out a breath. Every year his brothers-in-law put lights around the house while his dad cooked breakfast, which meant Brent watched six kids all by himself. He loved watching his nieces and nephews, but all together could be quite a challenge. "How 'bout I help Matt—"

"No. No." Nick lifted his hand and winked. "I got it."

As Nick left the house, Brent called back, "You better have changed Derek."

"He's good."

Brent shook his head as he walked into the living room. He hoped Matt had changed Brooke before he headed out to the shed. For now, all six kids were occupied. Ten-year-old Allie was braiding her eight-year-old cousin Hayley's hair. Five-year-old Ryan and four-year-old Ross played Legos on the floor, while two-year-old cousins, Derek and Brooke, sat together in the leather rocker watching a cartoon and sucking down juice in their sippy cups.

Brent got down on the floor with the boys and picked up a Lego block. "Can I play, too?"

The boys nodded, and Brent added his block to the base of their creation. "So, what are we building, boys?"

"A castle," said Ross.

"Nu-uh," said Ryan, "we're making a bridge."

"No, we not."

"Yes, we are."

Brent touched both of their shoulders before one or both of them started throwing blocks. "How 'bout we make a castle with a bridge."

Ryan snarled at his cousin, but Ross brightened. "Okay."

"Okay," Ryan relented.

A squeal sounded from Brooke, and Brent turned to see Derek yanking on a handful of her curls. "Derek, let go."

His voice was firm, and Derek's lower lip quivered then a wail exploded from within him. Brent stood and picked up Brooke to move her to the couch. He got a whiff of her dirty diaper and bit back a growl at his brother-in-law.

Holding her at arm's length, he went into the bedroom, found her diapers and wipes, and changed her. He could hear Hayley trying to console the crying Derek.

By the time he'd thrown the diaper in the trash outside and washed his hands, Ross and Ryan were fighting over their castle and bridge. Hayley was complaining that Allie had braided her hair too tight, while Allie growled that she'd never fix Hayley's hair again if she was going to whine. He looked at Derek and saw his face was red from strain. He knew in a matter of moments he'd have another stinky situation to deal with. "Dad, are the pancakes almost done?"

"Come and get it, everyone."

The children scampered into the dining room, and Brent begged Derek to hold the stink in until his dad got back inside. He made sure the kids got the pancakes they wanted since Dad fixed some with peanut butter, some with bananas, and some with chocolate chips. He poured orange juice for each of the children, and then his brothers-in-law walked inside.

Derek hollered, "I poop!"

Brent made a fist and pumped the air. "Yes! He waited until daddy got done." He lifted his hand, grabbed Derek's and lifted it up, then high-fived him. Derek giggled and Brent said, "Good boy!"

"Very funny," Nick grumbled.

Brent chuckled. "Hey, you said the boy was good, and I just agreed with you."

Nick lifted Derek out of the seat and took him back to the bedroom. Brent helped himself to a couple of banana pancakes. He sat beside Allie and pretended to take her plate. She swatted at him, and Brent laughed.

His dad settled into a chair across from him. "About time you have a few of these."

"What? Pancakes?" Brent teased.

His dad pursed his lips. "No, son. It's about time you settled down."

An image of Sabrina came to mind, and Brent pushed the picture from his brain. He should have thought of Carrie. "I'd like to, Dad. Just waiting on the right girl."

Nick walked into the room. "Laura said you've been dating someone."

"Yeah," Matt added, "some redhead. What was her name?"

"Carrie," Brent answered.

His dad raised his eyebrows. "You haven't mentioned her. What's she like?"

Brent added more syrup to Ross's pancakes then picked up the fork Ryan had dropped. After wiping the utensil off with a napkin, Brent shrugged. "Red hair, like Matt said. Nice girl."

His dad wrinkled his nose. "You don't sound all that interested in her."

"Yeah, Uncle Brent," Allie said, "you're supposed to say she's the most beautiful girl in the world, and you can't live another day without her."

Nick elbowed his oldest child. "Now, where did you hear all that?"

"Daddy, every girl knows that."

"Yeah," Hayley agreed.

Brent didn't respond. He didn't feel that way about Carrie. Not in the slightest. They'd been hanging out for a month, and he'd hoped his feelings for her would deepen, but they hadn't. He liked her. She was a nice woman and a fun friend, now that she'd allowed herself to act as she would with anyone else. But nothing else had changed. "You two eat your breakfast and stop being silly."

Once they'd finished eating, Brent helped his dad take

the plates back into the kitchen. "Dad, why don't you go rest your knee?"

"I will. Soon enough. I wanna hear more about this girl."

"There's nothing more to hear."

"That doesn't sound very exciting." His dad stacked the plates beside the sink. "Son, when I started dating your mother, I worked as hard and as fast as I could on the farm to get through my chores so I could drive into town to see her. I thought about her while I worked and dreamed about her when I slept. I hope you feel the same way about this redhead." He patted Brent's shoulder. "I think I'm going to go sit a while."

"You want some medicine?"

His dad opened his palm. "Already got some."

He watched his father as he tried to mask the limp as he walked into the living area. He didn't feel that way about Carrie. Truth be told, it was Sabrina who haunted his nights and who invaded his thoughts through the day. He wondered about her, worried about her, prayed over her. When he did see her, he feared his heart would beat right out of his chest.

He exhaled. He didn't want to think about this. Turning on the hot water, he rinsed the dishes and placed them in the dishwasher. He needed something to keep his mind off women. Brooke toddled into the kitchen holding a book in her hand. "Wead, Unc Bwent."

Brent picked her up and kissed her chubby cheek. She was a good diversion. "Of course, Uncle Brent will read you a book."

Sabrina hadn't felt so frustrated in a long time. She donned a pair of khakis and a navy button-down shirt. Today would be another work-behind-the-counter day at the coffee shop. She needed to keep her hands busy without overloading her brain. She'd read more of the Bible in the last few weeks since Thanksgiving than she had in her entire life. A lot of it made sense, but a lot didn't, too. And she just couldn't bring herself to have the faith the Bible talked about.

She walked into the coffee shop and spied Gretchen behind the counter. Happiness filled her at the sight of her friend. Gretchen walked around and gave her a hug. "You working with me today?"

"Yep."

"A lot on your mind again?"

"Yep."

"How's your sister doing?"

"Terrific. Even started dating the baby's daddy."

"But, you said—"

She lifted her hand to stop Gretchen from barreling her over with a bunch of questions. "I know. It's a long story. Turns out he's a Christian." Sabrina clasped her hands and lifted them to her chest. "Seems everywhere I go I'm surrounded by Christians."

Gretchen frowned. "That's a bad thing?"

"It is when you're trying to figure out how you feel about it all."

Gretchen nodded, a twinkle lit her eye. "I see." She grinned as she grabbed Sabrina's arm. "Well, get yourself on behind this counter and start making some coffee."

Sabrina chuckled as she followed Gretchen. She started a pot of caffeinated coffee then checked to be sure they had enough supplies. A lady ordered a grande mocha, and Sabrina started mixing it before Gretchen had a chance. She needed to stay busy.

Last night Jacob had come over after they heard the baby's heartbeat at the doctor's office. It was the first visit in which he'd accompanied Mallory. The look of excitement on his face twisted Sabrina's heartstrings. Mallory mentioned that Brent had been talking with both of them, and Sabrina had spent much of the evening thinking about Mallory's counselor. She didn't know what it was about the guy, but she wanted to see him again. Several times she'd been tempted to call him about the scriptures she'd read, but she'd stopped herself. She knew she needed to figure it out on her own.

Realizing they didn't have enough whipped cream, she went to the back of the shop, grabbed a case, and took it to the front. She looked up and saw Brent standing in front of the register. Her heart flipped in her chest, and a smile spread her lips.

When he saw her, a look of panic swept across his features. Then Sabrina noticed the woman standing beside him. She was tiny. In fact, they looked a little silly standing side by side. His head topped the girl's by more than a foot and a half. Red hair and freckles. She was cute but only moderately so. Sabrina could tell by the look of adoration on the woman's face as she stared up at Brent that she was more than just a work colleague.

Jealousy tugged at Sabrina's heart. He didn't need to be with the redhead. They didn't look good together. And what guy wanted a girl on his arm that looked at him like a puppy looks up at her master when he's holding a bone? Okay, so maybe just about every guy she'd ever met wanted to be idolized by his girlfriend. But didn't the Bible talk against that? She was pretty sure she'd read something like that recently. Brent didn't need some woman drooling all over him.

Gretchen said something, but Sabrina didn't catch it. She couldn't seem to tear her gaze from Brent and the girl with him. Why would he like a woman like her? She wasn't right for him.

"That's a black caffeinated and a french vanilla," said Gretchen.

Sabrina blinked and registered that she needed to make the coffees. Gretchen took the pastries they'd ordered from the glass counter, and Sabrina poured the drinks. Peering up at him, she almost laughed at the guilty expression on his face. Like he'd just gotten caught with his hand in his mother's cookie jar. She handed the cups to Brent. Her pinkie touched his, and Sabrina felt warmth heat her neck. She didn't understand her feelings toward him. It was probably good he was here with a woman. It would allow her to stop thinking about the Holy Roller so much.

He seemed to want to say something to her, but she turned away from him. He looked upset that she'd seen him with the girl, but there was no reason for that. There was nothing between them. She focused on putting the whipped cream in the refrigerator. *And you need to remember that, too, Sabrina. There is nothing between you and Brent.*

"Who was that?" asked Gretchen.

"Mallory's counselor."

"The one who gave you the scriptures?"

"Yeah."

Gretchen's mouth formed an O as she lifted her chin, obviously remembering the things Sabrina had said about Brent. She needed to learn to keep her mouth shut with Gretchen. The woman knew entirely too much about her, and what she didn't know for sure, she assumed. Didn't matter that her assumptions were often correct.

A sudden wave of emotion overwhelmed her, and Sabrina excused herself and went to the back of the store. A tear slipped down her cheek, and she swiped it away with the back of her hand. She had no reason to feel emotional.

She did not like Brent. Seeing him with another girl should not affect her at all. She swiped at a tear that fell from the other eye. Finding a box of tissue, she pulled one out and wiped both eyes. This was ridiculous.

She was tired. That was all. The last few months had been long ones, and the weight of all the responsibility she carried was finally starting to wear on her. She loved her sister, would do anything for her. But with each passing day and now that Mallory was starting to show, Sabrina fought battles from her past.

She longed to forget the miscarriage, not to think about what it must be like to feel a baby move inside her. What it would be like to hear her own baby's heartbeat, not just her sister's.

Why had God allowed her baby to die? She closed her eyes. She probably wouldn't have had the child anyway. The abortion was scheduled, and she wasn't as strong as Mallory when she was nineteen. She'd have listened to her parents. The truth of her weakness ripped at her heart. She should have been stronger. Should have been willing to stand up to them no matter what they said. She straightened her shoulders. She'd never allow herself to show such weakness again. She was in control of her life and all that happened in it. Never again would anyone dictate what she did or did not do.

"Sabrina, there's someone here to see you," Gretchen called from the front.

She gripped the tissue. Inevitably, Brent wanted to talk with her. Wanted to tell her…she had no idea what he'd want to say. She had no desire to talk with him, about his girlfriend, her sister, or anything. She sighed, but she might as well get it over with. She walked back to the front of the store. Surprise filled her. Brent wasn't standing behind the counter. It was the doctor from the emergency room from over a month ago.

Sabrina smiled. "Hi."

He grinned back. "You are one hard lady to track down."

Sabrina lifted her brow. "Really?"

He nodded. "I wonder if you'll make me a white chocolate mocha." He lifted a receipt. "I've already paid for it."

"Sure." Sabrina took her time and carefully fixed his hot drink. She put it on the counter. "There you go."

"I also wondered if you would be willing to join me for lunch." He pointed to Gretchen. "This lovely lady tells me you'll take a break in about an hour."

Sabrina grinned at Gretchen then looked back at the doctor. She drank in his gorgeous brown hair and eyes. He looked like the kind of man she usually dated. "Well, that depends."

"On?"

"Well, sir. I don't even know your name."

"That's an easy fix, *Sabrina*."

She smiled as he emphasized her name. He wanted her to know he'd remembered her. Pleasure traced through her veins. He extended his hand, and she drank in the kindness in his eyes. "I'm Mitch Isaacs. Now, will you have lunch with me?"

She grabbed his hand in hers. "I believe I will."

Chapter 10

Brent had to be honest with Carrie. He didn't care about her in the way he should. It wasn't fair to date her, hoping his feelings would change. When they'd run into Sabrina at the coffee shop, he'd felt dirty, like he was cheating on Sabrina with Carrie. In truth, it should have been the other way around. Carrie was his date. His feelings for Sabrina were wrong. He couldn't pursue the dark-haired beauty, but he couldn't date Carrie, either.

He sat in the booth across from Carrie. She looked pretty in a green dress, the sides of her red hair pulled up with a small green clip. She deserved a man who would cherish her.

She thumbed through the menu. "I'm not sure what I want to order."

"The steak is good."

He exhaled a breath. He'd decided to treat her to a nice dinner before telling her they couldn't continue seeing each other. Though it was the least he could do. Seeing her across from him, dolled up more than she usually was, he wondered if his logic had been the best.

She looked up at him, her eyes full of excitement and adoration. He felt like scum. She probably felt this was the first romantic date they'd had. What had made him think a nice dinner, romantic even, would be the best avenue to take to break it off with her? He should have never gone out with her. He'd battled his feelings for Sabrina each time they'd been together. He'd been selfish. *God, forgive me.*

He glanced back down at the menu, wishing the waitress would hurry up and get over here. He couldn't tell her at the table. Now that they were here, he at least owed her the dinner. But he didn't want to make goo-goo eyes at her, either. He trailed his finger against the edge of the menu. He'd really made a mess of this.

From the corner of his eye, he saw a tall, dark-haired woman following the hostess to a booth on the other side of the room. He looked over and sucked in a breath when he saw Sabrina in a red blouse and a short black skirt. High-heeled black boots hugged her calves all the way to the bottom of her knees.

A tall, dark-haired man followed her, and Brent's heart twisted in jealousy. The guy looked familiar. He wracked his brain trying to place him. Dawning hit. The doctor from the emergency room.

Swallowing the knot in his throat, he looked back at Carrie. She continued to study her menu, oblivious to his inner turmoil. "I think I will get the steak with the garlic parmesan on top."

"Sounds good." Brent couldn't think. He wanted to get out of here. Looking around the room, he bit back a growl. Where was their waitress?

He glanced back across the room, and his gaze locked

with Sabrina's. Her eyes widened in surprise. He nodded then looked away from her. He should wave, say hello, something, but he couldn't. Seeing her with someone else ripped at him from the inside. *I'm such a hypocrite. I'm sitting here with my own date.*

His father's words of how he felt for his mother trickled through his mind. He should have never asked Carrie out. Should have sought God. Listened to his gut. But he'd gotten caught up in wanting what his sisters and friends had—a happy marriage and children.

Brent was about to explode when the waitress finally arrived. Carrie ordered, and Brent decided to simply get the same. He didn't know what he wanted, didn't feel like eating. The night was going worse than he'd expected, and he'd anticipated it being right up there with the root canal he'd had a few years back.

He tried to focus on Carrie as she talked about her day at the office, but his gaze kept wandering to Sabrina and the doctor. His gut knotted when he saw her laugh at something the guy had said.

"I said 'how was your day?' "

Brent blinked and looked back at Carrie. "I'm sorry?"

"I've asked about your day twice."

Brent rested his arms on the table and clasped his hands. "I had a great day. Pretty easy, actually."

Carrie narrowed her gaze. "You seem a little distracted tonight."

Brent sighed. Maybe he should just tell her now. He opened his mouth to fess up, but the waitress appeared with their food. He said the blessing and they started to eat.

"This is really good. I'm glad you suggested it," said Carrie. She seemed to have forgotten her aggravation with him.

Brent nodded, glad he hadn't said anything. He'd wait

until they left. She chattered about the different ways to cook steak, and Brent tried to pay attention, tried not to notice when Sabrina laughed or when the guy touched the top of her hand across the table. Brent ate fast, praying God would get him through the dinner. When Carrie finished, he paid the bill and guided her out of the restaurant.

Sabrina didn't seem to have noticed him at all after she first walked in. He didn't know why his mind was so determined to think about her all the time. She didn't share his feelings. He didn't even want her to, unless she accepted Christ. Life would be so much easier if he could just like Carrie.

He shook his head. But he didn't. And he wouldn't lead her on anymore. He opened her car door then shut it behind her when she slipped inside. He was quiet on the drive home, trying to listen as she talked about her office's white elephant Christmas party. Once at her apartment, he walked her to the front door. Her eyes glistened as she looked up at him, and he realized she thought he was going to kiss her.

God, help. He exhaled a long breath and shoved his hands in his front pockets. "Carrie, I need to be honest with you."

She nodded, her expression still hopeful. He waited, pondering the best way to tell her the truth. She furrowed her brow. "What is it?"

He shifted his weight from one foot to the other. "The truth is I don't think this is working out."

"What?" She narrowed her gaze, and Brent cringed at the anger in her voice.

"It's just that—"

"We have fun together, don't we?" She placed her hands on her hips, and Brent noted she tapped her right foot against the sidewalk.

Brent nodded. "We do."

"Then what's the problem?" She smacked her hands against her thighs. Brent blinked. He'd never had a girl get riled up during a breakup. In his experience, their eyes glistened with tears and then they walked away. Course, he'd only experienced one other breakup where he was the one doing the dumping, instead of the one being dumped. But still. The woman had been looking at him with puppy-dog eyes all night, now she looked ready to bite him.

"That's just great, Brent. You take forever to finally ask me out. We have a great time together, and now you want to break it off."

Brent cocked his head. Was she remembering things right? Because he'd tried to go out with her and take her to dinner a few times before she actually went out with him. That should have been his hint. Especially since he wasn't really interested in her to begin with. He shook away his thoughts. There was no reason to argue with her about it. He simply needed to be honest. "I'm sorry, Carrie. You're a terrific woman, and I—"

She lifted her hand to stop him. "Save it." She yanked her apartment keys out of her purse and opened the front door. "Thanks for dinner."

Before he could respond, she stepped inside and slammed the door. He walked back to the car. He deserved her anger. Hadn't expected it, but her frustration was his own fault. He didn't care about her in the way a man should care for a woman. He hoped God would bring a good man into her life and a woman for him as well. Sabrina floated through his mind and he bit back a growl. Somehow he had to stop thinking about her.

Sabrina twisted the cloth napkin. Of all places and times to run into Brent! She'd fretted several times over seeing him at the coffee shop with the redhead. To run into him again tonight at the restaurant was too much. She'd tried to push thoughts of him away and focus on her date with Mitch, but Brent seemed to enjoy traipsing through her mind.

She shouldn't have been surprised to see Brent and the redhead here. It was a Friday night, and Greenfield was limited in its number of nicer restaurants. Still, what were the odds? And why did she care?

Sneaking a peek at her date, she drank in Mitch Isaacs' good looks. Mallory's nurse had probably been very accurate. Most likely every free woman in the hospital had the hots for the young doctor. Thick, dark hair that lay in perfect layers. Equally thick eyebrows over deep brown eyes. Not to mention the five o'clock shadow, which added the perfect amount of manliness.

And he'd gotten dressed up for her. Black jacket and pants. Starched white shirt and deep red tie. Unintentionally, they matched, and she knew they were a terrific looking couple. The glances they'd received from many of the other couples were proof enough. She bit the inside of her lip. But the peeks from Brent had unnerved her.

"So you're a district manager?"

Mitch's question broke her thoughts, and she smiled at him. She had a gorgeous date, and she had no intention of spending the rest of the evening worrying over her sister's counselor. She nodded. "Of sorts. I mainly deal with numbers and projections."

He pursed his lips and touched them with the tip of his fork. "I believe I stopped by that particular coffee shop ten times before I finally ran into you."

Sabrina bit her lip. "What do you mean?"

"Well, I knew you worked for the coffee chain, but the first time I visited that particular shop your friend,

Gretchen, told me you traveled to several of them. She suggested I stop in there for coffee before work and eventually I'd catch you."

Pleasure trailed through her at the thought of Mitch's persistence to meet her. He'd been a perfect gentleman the entire time. And she couldn't deny she'd enjoyed riding to the restaurant in his red Corvette. "Why didn't you just get my number from the hospital records?"

"Unethical." He winked, and Sabrina knew he'd been tempted to do just that. Maybe he even had but didn't use the information to call her. She liked that about him. Showed character. Or maybe it showed that he didn't want to lose his job if she thought he was a stalker and decided to press charges. She pushed back the insinuation. She had to stop being so cynical toward men.

She took a bite of her potato then nodded. "What about you? How did you end up in Greenfield?"

He set down his fork. "To be honest, I don't plan to stay here. It's a terrific start. I can get some experience. Hopefully work my way up in the surgical unit." He clasped his hands. "My goal is to go back to Nashville. Work in cardiology. When I was in my residency, I was able to work under an amazing heart surgeon. I plan to…"

Sabrina felt her eyes glazing over as he talked about the heart and the various surgeries he'd watched or helped perform. His passion was inspiring, but she didn't really care about the various vessels and arteries and capillaries and all the other gargantuan words he used. He was driven. That was for sure. Something she'd always appreciated in a man.

"That's enough about my job." He motioned toward her. "Tell me about your family."

She took a sip of her iced tea. "Well, my sister lives with me. She's a freshman in college, but you already met her."

"How is she doing?" The genuine concern in his gaze warmed her heart.

"She's doing very well. Thanks." She traced her finger around the edge of the glass. "My dad is actually a doctor, also."

"Really?"

She nodded. "He has a family practice here in town."

"Wait a minute." Mitch furrowed his brow. "You're Henry Moore's daughter?"

"I am." She wondered what her father's colleague thought of him. She'd always idolized her daddy as a little girl, until she learned he cared more about appearances and careers than he did about what was going on inside his daughters' hearts. She held back a huff. He probably also wondered why the town's doctor hadn't gone to the hospital to check on Mallory the night they thought she was miscarrying.

"Interesting."

Sabrina couldn't judge his response. She wanted to pry his opinion of her dad from him. Was he respected? Was he ethical? Was he a good doctor? She'd believed him to be a hero for so many years that when his true self was exposed she'd been devastated. "You probably already know my mom was a past state representative."

"I didn't. I've only met your dad in passing a few times." He reached over the table and grabbed her hand. His eyes had taken on a glazed look. "But I'm so glad I met you."

His hand was warm and soft in hers, but she hadn't felt the tingling she did when Brent touched her. She inwardly growled. She would not think about that counselor. She would think about her date. Smiling, she said, "I'm glad you were persistent."

"Me, too." He wiped his mouth with the napkin. "You are just the kind of woman I'm looking for."

Sabrina frowned. "What does that mean?"

"You know what it's like to have a doctor in the family. You know the long hours, and you have a career. You want to move forward in life, not just let it happen. Go out and reach for it. I want that."

Sabrina let his words fall on her. She remembered her father being gone most of her growing up years. Not all doctors were gone that much. The father of one of her friends was a doctor in her dad's office, and he went to most of her tennis matches. Sabrina's dad didn't.

She twirled a strand of hair. Since Mallory's pregnancy, Sabrina had been rethinking her life. She wanted to be there for her niece or nephew. She didn't want to be wrapped up in work and the pursuit of...what? An early grave from working herself into the ground? The loss of those she loved because she didn't spend time with them? Her personal goals were a lot to think about and now wasn't the time.

Mitch paid for their dinner. She stood, and he placed his hand in the small of her back and guided her to his car. He smelled wonderful, a soft, musky scent. There was strength and tenderness in his touch and an air of superiority in his walk. He was the man she'd always dreamed of. He would go places, and he wouldn't mind when she poured herself into her own career and goals. But something felt off. She didn't know if that life was what she truly wanted.

She pushed the thoughts away. The last few months had simply made her overly sentimental. All the baby stuff with Mallory and looking up all those scriptures Brent had given her. She needed to look at what was right in front of her. Think with her mind and not her emotions. Mitch was the man of her dreams. Literally.

He drove to her house and walked her to the door. He didn't pressure her or even suppose that he should go into the house with her. He simply kissed her cheek ever so gently. She remembered Jacob doing the same to Mallory and how she'd wanted that for herself. "I'd like to see you again."

Sabrina swallowed. He was so deliciously handsome. The perfect guy for her. Brent's surprised expression when their gazes had met in the restaurant flickered through her mind. She pushed thoughts of Brent away and smiled at Mitch. "That would be wonderful."

Chapter 11

Brent raked his hand through his hair. He had one hundred food baskets to fill. In only a few hours, he'd open the pantry doors and families would come for their Christmas fixings. Ivy'd had her baby boy a month ago and wouldn't be back. Carrie hadn't spoken to him since the night they'd had dinner. His other two volunteers were busy—one had her son's Christmas pageant to attend; the other had the flu. *God, I don't know how I can get these filled by myself.*

Sucking in a deep breath, he grabbed cans of green beans and started putting a can in each box. Ivy had been the organizer in the past. He'd followed her lead and lined twenty-five empty boxes along the wall. Once each was filled with the non-refrigerated foods, he'd fold the flaps in and place twenty-five boxes on top of them. Fill them up then make a row of twenty-five boxes in front of the boxes, fill them, close them, and repeat with the remaining twenty-five boxes. When a family arrived, he'd take a turkey and a frozen pumpkin pie from one of the freezers, open the box, put them inside, close it again, hand the box to the family, and then they'd be on their way.

He swallowed at the sheer amount of nonrefrigerated items that needed to be packed in boxes. Still, it was a simple procedure. He could do it. He had to.

His gut tightened when fifteen minutes had passed and he'd only managed to get the canned vegetables in the first twenty-five boxes. Less than two hours before he needed to be finished.

A knock sounded at the front door. He growled as he made his way to the front of the building. Surely no one would be here this early. He opened the door and smiled when he saw Will and Tab waving at him.

Tab grinned. "Thought you might need some help."

He opened the door wider. "How'd you know?"

She shrugged. "Carrie told me she never planned to set foot in this place again. Will said you were giving out food boxes today. I put two and two together."

Brent grabbed her in a bear hug. "You two are life-savers." He motioned for them to follow him to the back. After explaining the procedure, he glanced at Tab. "Carrie's still mad at me, huh?"

Will laughed. "You could say that. She spent an evening at our house talking about what a *great* guy you are."

Tab punched Will in the arm. "Hush." She looked at Brent. "She is a little sore. Said you kept making goo-goo eyes at some brunette when you were at dinner."

Brent felt his cheeks flush. He'd tried not to make his frustration with seeing Sabrina on a date so obvious. Although, he had admitted to God later that he was glad Sabrina had shown up. He'd spent the last several days focusing on his relationship with God, not worrying over women.

"Brunette, huh?" said Will. "Surely not the same girl you told me about weeks ago?"

Brent tried to ignore Will's comment as he placed empty boxes on the ones that had been filled and closed.

"What's he talking about?" asked Tab.

"Nothing." Brent scowled at his friend.

She tugged on his shirt. "Fess up."

Brent stretched his back then turned toward her. "There was a girl I was interested in, but she's not a Christian, so there's nothing more to tell."

Tab punched his arm. "Do you mean to tell me you went out with Carrie while you've been liking another woman?"

Will chuckled. "Yep."

"It wasn't like that." Brent shot Will a look of death. The man knew once Tab got going there would be no stopping her. She'd harp at him about this for the rest of his life. And he hadn't meant for the whole thing to turn out as bad as it had.

"Sounds like it was exactly like that," said Tab.

"Sabrina isn't a Christian. I had hoped…" He paused as he placed cans of corn in the boxes. He really didn't want to talk to Tab about this.

"Hoped what?"

"I had hoped my feelings for Carrie would change."

He placed the last row of boxes on top of the filled ones. Tab and Will didn't say anything else as they placed the food inside. Brent was thankful for the reprieve. He wouldn't have been able to finish had it not been for his friends, but he didn't want to talk anymore about Carrie or Sabrina.

"Looks like that's it," said Will, as he swiped his hands together.

"Wish we could stay and help you give them out," said Tab.

"Me, too," mumbled Brent. The rule regarding a background check for workers who distributed food was a good one; however, there were times when it was also a hassle for him.

Brent shook Will's hand then hugged Tab. "Thanks so much for your help. I couldn't have done this without you."

Tab patted his back. "I'm sorry it didn't work out with Carrie, and I'll pray about Sabrina."

Brent nodded. He didn't want to tell her that Sabrina had a boyfriend. A flashy doctor who was probably exactly the kind of guy she wanted. He walked them to the front door and opened it wide. Surprise washed through him when he saw Ivy standing outside, holding a car seat.

She grinned. "Distributing food boxes is my favorite part of the ministry. I couldn't miss it."

God, You've really taken care of me today. I couldn't have done it without some help. Brent motioned her inside then said good-bye to Will and Tab. He went back in the pantry and watched as Ivy lifted the small boy out of the car seat. She placed him against her shoulder. "I figured I'd take up the vouchers and you could grab the boxes."

He nodded. "Sounds like a good plan."

Though he liked it better long, Ivy had cut her blond hair into a short style. Her light blue eyes showed traces of fatigue beneath them. And yet, she was still beautiful. Motherhood agreed with her. "You want to hold him?"

Brent had always been a sucker for babies. He reached down and picked up the little guy. He had a head full of dark hair, like his dad. The baby was still so little, soft and smelling like lotion. Brent wanted this. A wife and a baby of his own.

He thought of Sabrina. She was nothing like the kind of woman he'd always planned to marry, and yet anytime he thought of the right woman for him, he thought of her. He handed the baby back to Ivy. "He's perfect."

She smiled. "Thanks."

The front door opened and the first family arrived. Brent waved at the two small girls who held their mother's hands, one on each side. The woman released the older one's hand and pulled the voucher out of her pocket. She handed it to Ivy, and Brent picked up a box, opened the flaps, and put a turkey and pie inside. He handed it to the woman. She smiled, exposing a missing front tooth. "Thank you."

He wondered about her life. "You're welcome."

Two more families arrived. The next few hours flew in a whirlwind. Brent was thankful. He'd wanted to shift his thoughts away from Sabrina. The busier he was, the better.

"It's a girl."

Mallory squealed, and Jacob and Sabrina grabbed her in a hug. Sabrina wouldn't have cared if the child had been a boy, but she'd secretly hoped for a little girl. She couldn't wait to buy dresses and hair bows.

"My mom's going to be so excited." Jacob kissed Mallory's forehead.

Mallory laughed. "With a house full of men, I suppose she will be thrilled."

Sabrina appreciated Jacob's tenderness toward her sister. She was proud of him that he'd gotten a full-time job at their local lumber distributor. Somehow, he continued to go to school full-time as well. His grades weren't as good as her sister's, but he was trying, and Sabrina couldn't fault him.

Sabrina turned toward the ultrasound technician. "We were afraid you wouldn't be able to tell since she's only fifteen weeks."

The woman shrugged. "Sometimes the kiddos hide, but not this one. She cooperated, and I got all the measurements I needed." She wiped the petroleum jelly off Mallory's stomach. "You're free to go. Dr. Coe will see you after the new year."

"Merry Christmas," said Mallory.

"You, too, sweetie."

The woman walked out of the room, and Mallory sat up and fixed her shirt. She smiled at Sabrina, tears glistened her eyes. "I'm so happy." She looked at Jacob. "Do you have the picture for your mom?"

He lifted the ultrasound printout. "Right here."

He took Mallory's hand and helped her off the bed. Sabrina's heart twisted. She was happy that his family had accepted Mallory and the baby. Her sister had started eating dinner with his family whenever Jacob wasn't working. Sabrina didn't want to be jealous, but part of her was. She didn't get to have her baby. Didn't have anyone happy about her pregnancy.

She blinked the thought away. Mallory's pregnancy hadn't been easy on her memories, but it hadn't been as difficult as she feared. In a strange way the pregnancy had been therapeutic. Or maybe the therapy came from the scriptures she'd been reading. Brent would probably say the scriptures were the reason. She hadn't planned on getting so wrapped up in the Bible. Part of her still felt like she was the only person she could truly depend on. But watching Mallory as she grew in her faith had caused a stirring Sabrina hadn't been prepared for.

Jacob took Mallory's hand in his as they walked to the car. "I wish I didn't have to work tonight. We'd celebrate."

"Don't worry. I'll take her to dinner." She looked at Mallory. "I thought we'd get some maternity clothes first. What do you think?"

Mallory nodded as she touched the hem of the University of Tennessee sweatshirt. "I am running out of clothes."

Jacob fished into his back pocket and pulled out his wallet. He took one hundred dollars out and handed it to Mallory. "It's all I have right now, but—"

Sabrina shook her head. "It's okay, Jacob. I'll buy them."

"No, I can take care of—"

"Jacob, I want to do this."

"So do I."

Sabrina stared at the kid. After all, that's what he was. Barely nineteen and trying to take care of a girlfriend and a baby. Sabrina noted the determination in his eyes, and her heart twisted. Her sister was a very fortunate girl. She blew out a breath. "Okay, but if it's more than that, it's on me."

He hesitated then nodded. Sabrina drove to the lumber distribution center where Jacob worked and dropped him off; then she and Mallory made their way to the mall. After purchasing four pairs of tummy-paneled pants and several shirts, Sabrina said, "So where are we going to eat?"

"Let's go by and invite Mom first."

Sabrina looked at her sister. She shook her head. "I'm not sure that's a good idea. We were just there Thanksgiving, and they pretended you weren't even pregnant." She nodded to her sister's belly. "You're showing a bit now."

Mallory lifted her hand to stop her. "I know. I've been praying about this. Either they accept me and the baby this time, or I'm going to leave them alone. I'll keep praying for them, but I won't try to get their approval."

Sabrina swallowed. Mallory sounded so old. When had her sister grown up? Actually, it was more than just adulthood and Sabrina knew it. Her sister was a new person. She'd just read something about Christians being a new creation in Christ. Sabrina hadn't decided if she believed all that the Bible had to say, but she couldn't deny the change in her sister.

While Sabrina drove, she sneaked a peek at her sister.

Mallory's eyes were closed and her lips were moving. She knew she was praying. It would probably take a lot of petitioning for their mother to react in the way that Mallory hoped. She pulled into the driveway and shut off the engine. "You ready?"

Mallory opened her eyes and nodded. "Almost." Sabrina watched as Mallory lifted the Tennessee sweatshirt over her head. She still wore a plain black, long-sleeved T-shirt, but her pregnancy was obvious. "Now I'm ready."

Sabrina followed her sister up the walk. They knocked on the door, and their mother opened it. She looked as beautiful as ever. Her hair, makeup, and nails fixed immaculately. She wore a Christmas green sweater and deep brown pants with brown high heels. A smile spread her lips; then she looked down at Mallory's belly. She frowned. "What do you girls want?"

Her tone was biting, and Sabrina grabbed Mallory's hand and squeezed. Sabrina was proud of her sister as Mallory straightened her shoulders and lifted her chin. "Today we found out I'm having a baby girl. Sabrina and I wondered if you'd like to go to dinner with us to celebrate."

Her mother squinted as she pointed a long, perfectly manicured finger at Mallory's stomach. "Mallory, do you plan to keep that baby?"

"I do."

"How do you plan to do that?"

Sabrina cleared her throat. She'd been too ashamed and weak to stand up for herself all those years ago. But not anymore. "I've already told you I will help her."

"Jacob, the baby's father, is also going to help," said Mallory.

Her mother laughed. "Sounds like you have it all worked out. I'm glad." She cut off her laugh and pierced them with a glare. "Because your father and I have worked too hard to allow this embarrassment in our lives."

Sabrina tightened her hold on Mallory's hand. "Mother—"

Her mom interrupted her. "I think the two of you need to make other plans for Christmas."

Before Sabrina could reply, she shut the door. Sabrina looked at her sister. Pain etched Mallory's features. "I'm sorry."

Mallory swiped a lone tear away. "Actually, it's okay. I won't try anymore. I'll pray and wait for them. God can do anything."

That was another scripture she'd read. Something about all things being possible with God. She bit back a laugh. God would be the only one who could change her parents' hearts.

Sabrina forced a smile. "So, where do you want to eat?"

Mallory laced her fingers through Sabrina's as they walked back to the car. "Thank you, Sabrina."

Sabrina furrowed her brow. "For what?"

"For sticking with me. For supporting me. You know I pray for you every day, too."

Sabrina nodded. She assumed as much. Once they reached the car, Mallory turned to her and grinned. "You know what I'm in the mood for?"

"What?"

"A big, fat, greasy hamburger."

Sabrina high-fived her sister. "My kind of girl, and I know just the place."

Chapter 12

Brent rushed toward the sanctuary. With the youth boys' Sunday school teacher away for Christmas, he'd agreed to teach their class. But discussion had gone longer than he'd expected, and now he was running late for the service. He hated to be late.

Grabbing a bulletin off the front table, he walked through the double doors on the left side of the church. Maybe it was good he was late. Will and Tab were visiting family, and he wasn't sure who he'd sit with. Possibly he'd hide out in the back.

He looked to his left and spied Sabrina sitting at the end of the last pew. She was alone. He wondered where Mallory was. Since people were still milling around, he leaned against a wall and waited to see if Mallory showed up. The church was huge. No one would pay attention to him anyway.

The music started and their worship minister made his way to the podium. He lifted both his hands. "Let's stand."

Sabrina stood. Mallory still hadn't arrived. Brent raked his hand through his hair. He wasn't sure what to do. He didn't want her to sit by herself, but he didn't want to torture himself by sitting with her, either. *Just go over there.*

The congregation started singing a praise song. He pushed away from the wall and walked toward her. She looked at him and smiled. Her expression seemed more vulnerable than he'd ever seen it, and his heart skipped a beat. "Hey, Brent," she whispered. "It's great to see you."

The sincerity in her tone twisted his gut. How he wished he didn't care so much for this woman. "Where's Mallory?"

"She went to church with Jacob."

His heartbeat raced. But Sabrina was here. By herself. God was working on her. Brent knew He was. He pointed beside her. "May I sit with you?"

"That would be great."

She scooted over, and Brent stepped into the pew. The song had changed, and Brent read the words to the contemporary Christmas song on the screen. He joined with the others, and within moments heard a soft soprano voice beside him. At first, Sabrina's voice was quiet; she barely mumbled the words. But as the song went on, she sang louder. *She has a beautiful voice, Lord.*

He tried not to focus on Sabrina but to focus on singing praises to the Lord. The music ended with a reminder from the music minister to shake someone's hand. Brent turned to Sabrina. "You have a beautiful voice."

She blushed. "Thanks."

Before he could say anymore, she shook hands with the person in front of her. Brent greeted the couple behind him then sat down. He sucked in a deep breath to calm his racing heart. *Remember the woman has a boyfriend. Just pray for her salvation.*

He felt as if he'd played a sick joke on himself, sitting beside her through the service. In vain, he tried to focus on the pastor who spoke of Jesus' birth and how He brought salvation to the world.

All Brent could think about was the light scent of Sabrina's perfume and how soft her hands looked sitting on top of the open Bible. He needed to get his head checked. Why would he subject himself to sitting beside her?

The service ended, and Brent turned to say good-bye. "Would you like to join me for lunch?"

Brent pursed his lips the moment the question came out. That was not what he meant to say. He needed to get away from the woman, to stop thinking about her. Not go to lunch with her.

"Sure."

She smiled, and Brent wished he were a stronger man. He shoved his hand in his front pocket and pulled out his car keys. "Where would you like to go?"

"The deli on the corner okay?"

Carrie walked by glaring at him and Sabrina. He grabbed Sabrina's arm, praying Carrie didn't say anything, and guided her to the car. Once at the deli, they ordered sandwiches and sat at a small table against one of the walls.

"Was that redheaded girl your girlfriend?" asked Sabrina.

Brent shook his head. "No. We went on a few dates, but she was never my girlfriend." What would she think of him if he admitted he'd gone out with Carrie so he could stop thinking about her? He hated that he'd done that to Carrie. He couldn't blame her for scowling every time he came into the room. Tab assured him that once she met a new guy, Carrie would forget all about it. Brent still hated that he hadn't been honest from the beginning. With himself, even. "You dating the emergency room doctor?"

She bit her bottom lip, and again Brent wished he'd just kept his big mouth shut. It wasn't his business. Sabrina had no idea that she made his brain whirl with stupidity and his heart practically beat out of his chest. If she did, she'd probably run out of the deli and never look back.

She looked at him. "No. We went out the one time." She rested her arms on the table. "He's exactly like the guys I usually date, but…" She glanced up at him. "I don't know." She leaned forward. "When did you become a Christian?"

Warmth flooded him at the obvious battle going on inside her. God was working on her heart. *Please, God, keep nudging.* The memory of his salvation washed over him, and he grinned. "When I was ten. I was swimming in my friend's backyard after church. The preacher had talked about repentance and how we've all sinned against God."

He chuckled at the memory. "I wasn't supposed to be at my friend's house. My parents had gone to the store, and I wasn't supposed to leave the house."

Sabrina's eyes glistened as she listened to him. She hung on his every word, and Brent found himself falling more for her. "What happened?"

"I started feeling guilty. Knew what I was doing would not only make my parents mad but also upset God."

"What did you do?"

"I got out of that pool, raced back to my house and into my room. I flopped on the bed, started crying, and asked God to forgive me. To save me."

"Just like that? No church?"

"Just like that." His spirit stirred, and he reached across the table and grabbed her hand. "Accepting Christ isn't a churchy thing. It's a relationship thing. It's about what's going on with you and God."

Sabrina studied him for a moment. He prayed she would

see truth. She looked down at her plate. Pulling her hand away, she picked up the sandwich. "This is really good."

Brent held back his frustration. He wanted her to become a Christian, but she had to accept Christ in her own time. He nodded. "Yes. I've eaten here several times. Haven't gotten a sandwich I didn't like."

They finished their lunch, and Brent guided her back to the car. He'd wanted her to pray for salvation. Right then and there in the deli shop. Pulling out on the street, he tried to not allow frustration to take hold of him. He'd prayed so hard and so much for her. God heard his prayers, but...

He blinked. The light in the intersection turned red. Where had the light come from? He hadn't noticed it. Wasn't paying attention. He slammed the brakes. Stretching his arm across the passenger seat, he had to protect Sabrina. Too late. A horn blew and everything went black.

Confusion washed over Sabrina as she opened her eyes. She glanced down at her body. Pieces of glass covered her shirt and pants. Her hands shook and her collarbone screamed. She looked to her left. Panic swelled within her. Rivers of blood streamed down Brent's head. She pushed his arm. "Brent! Brent!"

What had happened? She couldn't remember. They were in a car. "Please, Brent!" He didn't answer. Tears welled in her eyes and spilled down her cheeks. She shoved him harder. "Please!"

"Don't move him, honey."

An older woman suddenly stood by his door. She put her hand through the window and touched his wrist. Where had the glass come from? Sabrina took in the pieces scattered all over the place—on Brent, the dash, the gears, on her. What had happened?

"It's okay, sweetie. It's going to be okay."

Another older woman stood beside her. The car door was open. When did the woman open it? Sabrina was confused; her neck hurt and her collarbone screamed.

The woman beside her unbuckled the belt. She placed her hand in Sabrina's. "Are you okay?"

Her mind cleared, and she remembered the light. It was red. Brent didn't stop. He stretched his arm across her. There was a horn. Then the crash of metal against metal. She looked at Brent again, and the tears fell faster. He was covered in blood, and the door was smashed into his leg. She grabbed his hand. "Please don't die."

"He's not dead, honey," said the woman beside his door. "His heartbeat is strong, and the ambulance will be here in a minute."

She looked past the woman. A man stood beside a white car. He was talking to the person inside. The car was smashed up against the front of Brent's car. She pointed to the other car. "Are they all right?"

The woman smiled. "I think so, honey. God was looking out for you all."

God. God was looking out for them.

Sirens sounded from the distance. Brent still hadn't awakened, and even though the woman said he was alive, Sabrina wanted to get him to the hospital. The paramedics arrived and a short man came up beside her. He took her hand and helped her out of the car. He asked her questions, and she replied, but she didn't know what she said. She couldn't take her eyes off Brent.

Fear filled her as they used a machine to pull the door away from him. She sat in the back of the ambulance, waiting for them to bring him to her. He never woke up. *Please, God. He has to be okay.*

Nausea welled inside her. Sabrina leaned over and vomited.

"I'm taking her in to check for internal damage," the short man said to someone else.

Sabrina shook her head. She didn't want to leave Brent. She had to be there when he woke up. Had to see that he was okay. Her stomach churned, and she threw up again.

A younger woman maneuvered her onto the stretcher in the back of the ambulance. The doors shut before Sabrina could protest, and she felt the wheels moving beneath them.

"Brent," she said.

The woman patted her hand. "He'll be with you before you know it."

Tears streamed down her cheeks, and her chest trembled from crying. She didn't want Brent to die. She didn't want to die. *If I die, I won't go to heaven.*

Fear overwhelmed her as she thought of Jesus and who she was in relation to Him. She'd sinned so many times in her life. Done so many things against God's will. Jesus wanted to save her. She knew He tugged at her heart, even at that moment. All she had to do was surrender. Give up control.

Sobs overtook her, and Sabrina gasped at the pain in her neck and chest. She'd done a mediocre job at best when it came to controlling her life. Spent most of her adulthood bitter—with her parents, with the miscarriage, with men. She yearned for freedom, for the chance to allow someone else to be in charge. She needed Jesus. *Forgive me, Lord. Come into my heart. Save me.*

Peace flooded her soul, and Sabrina sucked in a deep breath to calm her sobs. The ambulance stopped, and the doors flew open. They wheeled her down the hallway and into a room. In moments, they took X-rays of her and cleaned the small cuts on her face, neck, and left arm from the flying glass.

She wanted to see Brent. Needed to know he was all

right. The doctor came into the room. He was older, looked familiar. Did he work with her dad? He was smiling. "You'll be okay. No breaks. No internal bleeding. But for a few days you'll probably feel like you've been run over."

"Brent?"

"He's okay. His family is already with him."

"Please, may I go?"

"Sure, but let's do this." He helped her to her feet then set her in a wheelchair. "Nurse Sherry will take you to him. Stay in the chair."

She wouldn't argue. Her body ached, and she still didn't trust herself not to throw up—even if she did feel a peace she'd never before known. Nurse Sherry wheeled her into Brent's room then left to check on another patient. A couple who had to be his parents stood by the bed. A woman a few years older than Sabrina stood on the other side. Sabrina looked at Brent. He had a bandage above his left eye, but he was awake.

Relief swelled within her, and new tears streamed down her cheeks. "You're okay."

"Sabrina." He pressed both hands against the bed then winced against the effort.

"You stay put, son," said the man Sabrina assumed to be his dad. "You've got broken ribs and a broken leg. A concussion—"

"But he's alive," said the woman who must be his mother.

"And you'll be okay?" Sabrina asked.

"I'll be okay now that I know you're fine." He shook his head. "I'm so sorry, Sabrina."

"It was an accident."

"Yes," said his mother, "and the man in the other car walked away from the wreck."

His dad clicked his tongue. " 'Course the insurance—"

His mom elbowed him in the arm. She walked toward Sabrina with her hand extended. "We haven't properly met. I'm Mary, Brent's mother." She pointed to the man. "This is his dad, George." She nodded to the other woman. "And that's his sister, Laura."

Sabrina still felt dazed and a little confused, but she also felt peace and contentment. Thankful that Brent was alive, that she was okay and would be for all of eternity. She shook each of their hands. "It's my pleasure to meet all of you."

"You're sure you'll be fine?"

Sabrina looked back at Brent. Agony twisted his features, and she knew it wasn't simply from the physical pain he felt.

Laura motioned to her mom and dad. "Let's let them talk a minute."

His mother hesitated; then she nodded and took George's hand. Sabrina waited until they left the room. Though the doctor would probably fuss at her if he walked in, she stood and made her way carefully to his bed. She sat on the right side and took his hand in hers. "I'm better than I was before the accident."

Brent frowned. "What do you mean?"

She smiled and tears welled in her eyes again. Her eyelids would swell shut if she didn't get a handle on the waterworks, but she didn't care. She swiped away the tears with her free hand. "I accepted Christ."

Brent pressed his head against the pillow and closed his eyes. "You have no idea how much I've prayed for you."

Sabrina leaned over and kissed his cheek. "It worked."

Chapter 13

Brent sat up on his parents' living room couch and grinned at his dad. "Looks like you got all healed up from your knee surgery just in time."

"Just in time for what?"

He lifted his empty glass and waved it back and forth. "To start waiting on me."

His dad huffed and folded his arms in front of his chest. Brent knew the grumpy expression on his dad's face was a facade. The wreck had scared his parents, and he'd caught both of them standing over his bed praying aloud for his healing when they'd thought he was asleep. He didn't mind the prayers, as he felt as if he'd been run over by a semitruck. Breathing hurt. Pain shot through his leg. And the headaches were almost unbearable. But it was Christmas, and he was determined to enjoy it with his family.

"I'll get it for you, Uncle Brent," said Allie. She hopped up and grabbed the glass from his grip. "You want eggnog?"

"That sounds delicious."

Christmas had been a challenge for his nieces and nephews since he couldn't roughhouse with them. It had been hard for him as well. He hated having to lie still to allow his ribs to heal and keep his leg propped up because of the break. He knew a week from now his ribs would feel much better and he'd be able to get around easier, even with the cast on his leg. But for now, he felt like a crippled mess.

His mom handed him a bottle of water and two pills. "Time for your medicine."

He took them from her. "Thanks."

His sister Lisa curled her legs underneath her in the chair across from him. "So tell me about this Sabrina. Laura said she's quite a looker."

Allie came back into the room with more eggnog than he'd be able to drink. "Here you go, Uncle Brent."

He took the glass. "Thanks, Allie." He looked back at his sister. "Well—"

The doorbell rang, and his mom jumped up to answer it. "Hello. It's wonderful to see you again."

"We brought some cookies for Christmas, and my sister—"

Brent raised his eyebrows at the sound of her voice. He tried to sit up, but the pain in his left side kept him down.

Lisa grinned. "Looks like I'm going to get to meet her right now."

Brent watched as his sister stood and moved to the front door. He could hear the introductions. Sabrina's faint laughter filled his heart. She was a Christian now. He was free to fall in love with her.

Mallory walked in front of him. Her belly had grown quite a bit in the last few weeks, and she looked a bit swollen. A little early for that, but he figured it was simply because she'd been so thin to begin with. She smiled. "How you doing, Brent?"

He grinned back at her. "Doing all right. I've been better."

"They're going to miss you at the center."

"Tell me about it. Four weeks, at least. I'll probably go crazy."

"But you'll do exactly what they tell you."

Brent looked toward Sabrina's voice. His heartbeat raced at the sight of her. She still had some cuts on her forehead and jaw, even had a small bruise on her cheekbone, but she was the most beautiful thing he'd seen all day. All of his life. He nodded. "I will. How was your Christmas morning?"

"Quiet."

Mallory huffed. "I tried to get her to go to Jacob's with me, but she wouldn't do it."

Had she spent the whole day by herself? It was well past dinner. The idea of her being alone on Christmas broke his heart. Mallory told him about the visit to their parents' house, how their parents had uninvited them for Christmas. Sabrina should have spent it with him. He'd missed her all day.

"Don't let her make it sound like that. I enjoyed making all kinds of things. Including cookies for you all," said Sabrina. "And I soaked in a hot tub and took a couple of naps."

"Yeah. Her collarbone looks disgusting. It's all black and purple."

Guilt weighed him. If he'd been paying attention, she wouldn't be bruised up, and he wouldn't be flat on his back.

"If you ladies don't have anywhere to go, you could hang out with us awhile," said Laura.

"Oh yes, my grandchildren will be putting on their play in just a little bit," said his mother.

Sabrina lifted her eyebrows. "A play?"

"It's tradition," said his dad.

Brent explained, "Every year the kids make up some sort of skit and perform it for us. If they do a good job, Mom gives them a bag of homemade candy."

Sabrina smiled. "I'm assuming they always do a good job?"

His mother winked. "Always."

Brent watched as Sabrina and his family talked. She seemed comfortable with them, and he could tell they liked her. He wished he could get off the couch and sit beside her. He wanted to hold her hand, to feel its softness. To press his lips against hers, to rake his fingers through her hair. He blinked. *Get a grip, man. She'd run out of here if she knew what you were thinking.*

The wreck had scared him. What if he'd killed her? Or the other driver? Life was precious, and he didn't want to waste any more time. No more games. No more trying to feel things he didn't or trying to stop feelings that were happening. He wanted to tell her how he felt about her. A pain sliced through his brain, and he squinted. He also wanted to close his eyes, to sleep until the ache in his head went away.

Hayley walked down the hall and announced the play was ready. He swallowed, begging the pain to subside for just a little longer. Within moments, Derek and Brooke sat on the floor beating wooden spoons against the carpet. Ryan and Ross came into the room doing cartwheels. Hayley said the Pledge of Allegiance, and Allie sang "The Star Spangled Banner."

Brent whispered, "Not once have these kiddos made their play about Christmas."

Sabrina covered her mouth to keep from giggling, and Brent exhaled. After his mother passed out their bags of candy, Sabrina stood up. "I hate to leave, but I have to work in the morning."

Brent pursed his lips. He didn't want her to leave, but the pain in his head was mounting. He knew at any moment he would lose the battle and fall off into dreamland. "I'm glad you came by."

She wrung her hands together and shifted her weight from one foot to the other. "I was wondering if you'd be willing to help me study my Bible."

He couldn't imagine why she acted nervous. He'd do anything she asked. "Of course. Come over any time you're able. I'm stuck for a while."

Sabina nodded. "Okay." She bent down and kissed the top of his head. When she stood up, he could see she had something she wanted to say. She opened her mouth; then her expression shifted and she smiled. "Don't try to do anything. Let yourself heal."

"Oh, he doesn't have a choice," said his mother.

He waved to Mallory, and his mom walked them to the door.

Lisa grinned like a Cheshire cat. "I like her."

Brent adjusted the pillow beneath his head. "I'm glad."

"I think *you* like her, too."

Brent shrugged. He wouldn't deny it. Not anymore. Life was too short, and once he was healed, he would pursue her. Doctor or no doctor.

"I think she likes you, too."

Brent closed his eyes, as sleep invaded his brain from every angle. He prayed his sister was right, because he'd already lost his heart to Sabrina.

* * *

A little over a week had passed since the accident. Sabrina's cuts and bruises were mostly healed, except for the big bruise on her collarbone. She'd received flowers and texts from Mitch, but she hadn't replied. She just couldn't. God had been her focus. Spending time in His Word. Learning His will for her life. Mitch wasn't who she needed, and she'd have to tell him. Soon.

She'd talked with Brent a few times on the phone but not for long. His pain got more intense the first few days after the accident, and she wanted to give him time to heal. She also wanted to give herself time to think about her feelings for him.

She walked into the coffee shop and smiled when she spied Gretchen adding whipped cream to a beverage. The only contact she'd had with her older friend since before Christmas had been the flowers Gretchen had sent and the Facebook message stating that she prayed Sabrina healed quickly.

Gretchen handed the coffee to the patron and then noticed Sabrina. She opened her arms as she walked out from behind the counter and toward Sabrina. "Well, don't you look the most peaceful I've ever seen you." Gretchen wrapped her arms around Sabrina. "I'm so glad you're okay."

Sabrina released her friend and peered into her eyes. "I'm more than okay."

"I can tell that. You have news for me?"

"I got saved."

Gretchen wrapped her arms around Sabrina again. "I knew it." She squeezed. "Praise God."

Sabrina untangled from her friend, and they walked back behind the counter. "I'm supposed to be off today, but I wanted to spend it with you." She looked at her cell phone. "Well, maybe just a few hours. Mallory has an appointment with Dr. Coe this afternoon."

"You know I'll take you anytime I can have you."

A customer walked into the shop, and Sabrina made the girl a frappé. How one could drink a frozen beverage when it was below zero outside was beyond Sabrina, but she wouldn't argue with the customer.

It felt good to be behind the counter, to take orders, and fix drinks. She'd been making more pastries and desserts at home also, which Mallory and Jacob were all too willing to gobble up. Lately, she'd found herself less content crunching numbers and writing projections for the coffee shops across part of the state.

The change of interest shouldn't have come as a surprise. In the past, anytime she was stressed, she'd come into the coffee shop on her day off and work with Gretchen. She'd always assumed it was solely to get her mind off her stress, to do something with her hands that didn't require a lot of thinking. But Sabrina was beginning to realize the desire was more than that. She enjoyed the work of concocting a flavored coffee or mixing and baking some kind of treat. Crunching numbers and writing reports were not as much fun anymore.

She'd been thinking and praying a lot about that lately. What God wanted from her. What kind of work He'd created her to do. She wouldn't make any rash choices. Her faith was new, and she still didn't understand a lot of what she read in the Bible. But her outlook had changed. She was willing to follow wherever He led.

"What a surprise to see you here."

Sabrina looked up at the sound of Mitch's voice. Warmth traipsed up her neck and cheeks. She'd been rude not to text him back. At the very least, she owed him a thank-you for the flowers he'd sent. "I got your flowers. They were beautiful. Thank you so much."

Concern etched his features, and Sabrina felt like an even bigger heel. "How are you feeling?"

"I'm doing well. Only had a few cuts and bruises, and the soreness is almost gone."

"That's good. I texted you, but you never responded."

Sabrina looked over her shoulder at Gretchen. She noticed the woman seemed to work feverishly at scrubbing a bowl in the sink. Even so, she knew her dear friend paid attention to every word said. "Gretchen, I'll be right back."

Her friend nodded, and Sabrina motioned for Mitch to follow her to one of the tables. He sat down and she sat across from him. Realizing she hadn't made him a coffee, she gasped. "I'm sorry, Mitch. I didn't get your drink."

"I hadn't ordered one."

Sabrina lifted her hand. "Let me get it for you. White chocolate mocha, right? I'll get it."

He shook his head, but Sabrina slipped out of the chair and headed back behind the counter. Her hands shook as she prepared his drink. *Please, God. Give me the right words to say.*

She almost laughed out loud. A few months ago she would have had no trouble using her words to slice a man to the quick if she didn't want to date him. Her cheeks warmed at the arrogance she'd displayed in the past. *And the irony is Mitch would have been the man I'd have married, if I hadn't accepted You, Lord.*

An image of Brent waltzed through her mind. When she'd first met him, she'd viewed him as someone beneath her, someone who needed to get a grip on the real world. Now she wanted to know him better. Much better.

She popped the lid on Mitch's coffee then walked back to the table. She handed it to him, and Mitch looked at his watch. "I don't have a lot of time, Sabrina. I have to be at work in thirty minutes."

"I'm sorry I didn't text you. I…" What should she say? Should she tell him about her new faith? He'd probably think her an idiot. She would have a few months ago. "I've changed." She swallowed, silently asking God to help her. Why was it so hard to talk about Him when He had saved her life? Literally. "I've become a Christian, and I'm learning that—"

He wrinkled his nose and shook his head. "What?"

She placed her arms on the table, clasping her hands. "My priorities…what I want. They're not the same. I—"

Mitch raised his hand to stop her. "I've heard enough. I thought you would be a great fit. Your dad even seemed pleased… ."

Sabrina sat up straighter when he mentioned her father. Mitch had talked to her dad about them? They'd only been on one date.

He waved his hand. "But I don't have time for all this. I have things I want from life. Goals I plan to achieve." He extended his hand.

Surprised by his abruptness, she grabbed his hand and shook it.

He nodded. "It was a pleasure meeting you, but we obviously have different ideas about life."

Unable to respond, Sabrina watched as he stood and walked out of the coffee shop. His words settled into her mind. He'd spoken the complete truth. A year ago, she and Mitch would have made the perfect pair. They'd have conquered the world together.

But things had changed. She no longer wanted to conquer the world. She wanted to live in it. To love in it. To redeem it. She wanted to see God, to know Him, and to show Him to others. She didn't have to be on top of the world. She didn't have to climb the success ladder at the expense of anyone who got in her way. God had changed her, and she would follow wherever He led. Right now, she longed to see Brent.

Chapter 14

Brent felt as though he was going crazy. He'd been cooped up in his parents' house for three weeks. His ribs felt much better—still sore when he coughed and he had to be careful not to stretch his arm all the way over his head—but the headaches were gone, and he was ready to get back to work. Back to life.

The snowstorm the week before hadn't helped. Sabrina had visited every day or two before then. They'd shared scriptures and stories about their childhoods and what they wanted from life. But because of slick roads, it had been a week since he'd seen her. He didn't know how much more separation he could take.

His mother stood up and pointed to the kitchen. "Wanna help with the dishes?"

He bit back a growl. He did not want to help with the dishes. But he knew his mother was just trying to help. She knew he was stir-crazy and needed to do something to occupy his time. Maybe if he was a reader, he wouldn't be so antsy. He'd tried reading some of his dad's westerns, but they'd bored him nearly to tears.

He pushed off the couch. "Sure."

Hobbling on his walking cast, he followed his mom into the kitchen. She scraped pans and wrapped up lunch leftovers while he rinsed off the dishes and placed them in the washer. Looking out the back window, he saw his dad shoveling the driveway. He wished he could help his dad, not be stuck in the kitchen. His parents hadn't been able to leave the house, either. He watched his dad shovel. His dad grew every bit as impatient as Brent when he was cooped up too long, which meant his parents must be planning to head to town. "You and Dad going somewhere today?"

"Thought we'd run to the store. Maybe grab some dinner."

He nodded. And he'd be stuck here alone. Letting out a sigh, he couldn't blame them for wanting to get out of the house. He had to find something to do. He'd completed every crossword puzzle and sudoku game in the place.

A knock sounded at the front door. He lifted his brows, wondering who that could be. Probably Lisa. She and Matt lived just a little way down the country road. His mother most likely asked her to come babysit him while she was gone. Rolling his eyes, he continued arranging dishes in the washer, while his mother went to answer the door.

"Now that's something I've never seen before."

He turned at the sound of Sabrina's voice. His heart skipped at the sight of her. Her brown eyes twinkled with merriment. Her long dark hair fell in a straight mass down her left shoulder. She wasn't dolled up like when he'd first met her. She wore just a little makeup and a black jumpsuit. He grabbed a towel off the counter and wiped his hands. "What? You've never seen a man washing dishes?"

"Never."

He grinned and opened his arms. "It's good to see you."

She walked toward him and gently wrapped her arms around him. The floral scent of her shampoo made him light-headed. He inhaled a deep breath before she let him go. His arms felt empty when she stepped back. He wanted her to stay there. Close to him. Forever.

His mother wrapped her arm around Sabrina's shoulder. "I'm so glad you're here, sweetie. Makes me feel better about leaving him."

Brent pursed his lips. "Is that why you were acting weird? You were worried about leaving me? Mom, I'm twenty-eight years old."

Sabrina raised her eyebrows. "Almost twenty-nine, I heard. On Valentine's Day."

His mother placed her hand against her chest. "Ever since the day that boy was born I've said that he'd always be my Valentine."

Laughter shone in Sabrina's eyes as she grinned at him, and he knew she'd tease him about his mother's words later. He scowled at the woman who'd given him birth. "Mom!"

His mom swatted the air. "Oh honey, she knows I'm just teasing you." She looked at Sabrina and lifted her brows. "When is your birthday, sweetie?"

"Mine was in October."

"How old are you?"

Brent wanted to crawl under the table. "Mom, you don't ask a woman her age. You're a woman! You should know that."

Sabrina laughed. "I don't mind." She turned to his mom. "I'm thirty-one."

"You're the same age as Lisa. You must have graduated the same year."

Sabrina twisted her silver ball earring as she shifted her weight from one foot to the other. "We wouldn't have known each other. My sister and I went to private school."

His mom looked at him. "Honey, this is the first older woman you've brought home."

His jaw dropped and he stared at her. "Mother."

Innocence wrapped her expression, and he knew she had no idea how impossibly embarrassing she was behaving. He felt like he was in middle school all over again.

His dad walked in the door. "Mary, you ready?"

Brent breathed a sigh of relief. *Get Mom out of here before she says anything else.* It amazed him that even after twenty-eight years the woman still managed to embarrass him to the core of his being. His mom left the room to grab her coat, and he shrugged at Sabrina. She chuckled, and his mom came back in the room. She kissed Sabrina's cheek. "Take care of him for me."

Sabrina winked at Brent. "I will."

Brent hobbled to his mother and kissed the top of her head. "Go have fun with Dad. I'm fine."

She and his father waved good-bye and left the house. He stared at Sabrina. It was the first time he'd been alone with her since she accepted Christ. Everything in him wanted to sweep her in his arms and kiss her until there was nothing left in him. Instead, he cleared his throat.

She pointed to the counter. "I brought some goodies."

He shifted his gaze. He hadn't noticed the tray of cookies and cream puffs. He hobbled toward her. "Yum." He pulled off the cellophane and popped a cream puff into his mouth. "Delicious."

She looked up at him. "So what do you want to do today?"

Kiss you. He swallowed back the words before they left his mouth. Her expression was tender and open, and he believed she was willing to accept what he wanted. Her gaze moved to his lips, and Brent thought he might lose his balance.

He leaned toward her. He hadn't kissed a woman in years. But he'd dreamed of Sabrina's lips. They'd taunted him. Haunted him. Now he'd feel them against his own.

The doorbell rang.

Brent blinked and looked past her toward the front door. Who could possibly be here now? And what horrible timing. A blush trailed up Sabrina's neck, and he wished he could feel its warmth with his lips. Pushing the thought away, he made his way to the front door. He peeked outside then opened the door wide. "Hey! What a surprise."

Tab and Will walked into the house. They took off their coats, and Tab took Will's from him. "Brent, where can I put—" She stopped when she spied Sabrina. "Oh, hi." She extended her hand and walked toward Sabrina. "I'm Tab, and my guess is you're Sabrina."

Sabrina grabbed her hand. "You're right. It's a pleasure to meet you."

Will leaned toward Brent and whispered, "Dude, you were right. She is hot."

Brent elbowed his friend. "Hush. She'll hear you. What are you two doing here?"

Tab set her purse on the end table. "We dropped the kids off at his parents' house. Figured you were about to go crazy stuck here in the house for the past few weeks." She pulled out a deck of cards. "Thought we'd play Rook." She looked at Sabrina. "Course I thought his mom would be the fourth player. She loves to play—"

"I love Rook," said Sabrina.

Brent cocked his head. "But are you any good?"

Sabrina lifted one eyebrow at him and then glanced at Tab. "You wanna play boys versus girls?"

Tab laughed as she lifted her hand for a high five. "If that's your answer to Brent's question, then yes, I do."

Sabrina smacked Tab's hand then motioned for them to follow her into the kitchen.

Will leaned toward him again. "She already knows her way around your parents' house? When's the wedding?"

Brent chuckled as he patted his friend's back. "Come on, man. Looks like we're about the get our rears kicked."

Will shook his head. "I don't even argue about it anymore. Just take the rear whipping like a man."

Brent laughed as they followed the girls into the kitchen.

"That's right," Tab said, "gotta train them right, early on."

"Well, Brent was doing the dishes when I walked in." Sabrina winked at Brent, and his heart flipped in his chest again. He'd do the dishes, let her win, whatever she wanted. He was wrapped around her little finger. Completely smitten. And he didn't even mind admitting it.

While Sabrina put the snacks she'd brought on the table, Brent grabbed soft drinks from the refrigerator. Tab set up the game. Brent sat down and Will sat across from him. The girls took their places. Sabrina scooped up the deck of cards and started shuffling like a professional dealer. Brent grimaced. "I have a feeling we're in trouble, friend."

Will nodded. "Yep. Looks like it."

In a matter of moments, Tab and Sabrina had cleared through the first round, claiming an easy win. Tab lifted her fist across the table, and Sabrina knuckle-bumped it. Brent rolled his eyes. "Seriously, girls?"

Sabrina's eyes lit with mischief. "Don't be a sore loser, Brent."

Tab leaned toward Will. She grabbed his cheeks with both hands and then kissed his mouth. "You don't care if I beat you, do you?"

Brent raised his eyebrows. He wouldn't mind, either, if Sabrina leaned over and planted a big kiss on his lips. He glanced at Sabrina and bit back a laugh at the bright pink color spreading her cheeks. *Was she thinking the same thing?*

They continued to play, and after losing four games in a row, Brent lifted up a white napkin and waved it. "Mercy. I call mercy."

Sabrina stood, reached across the table, and shook hands with Tab. "Great job, partner. But I better get going."

"Let's do it again soon," said Tab.

Brent walked Sabrina to the front door. He hated to see her go, but he didn't want her driving the snow-ridden country roads at night, either. "Thanks for coming."

"That was a lot of fun. Your friends are really nice."

He nodded. He wanted to kiss her, wanted to ask her on a date, wanted so much, but he just couldn't conjure the words. She lifted her hand and touched his cheek. Brent sucked in a breath. "I'll see you soon."

Before he could lean down to claim her lips, she walked out the door. He watched her until she made it to her car and drove away. The next time he saw her, he wouldn't be timid or nervous. He'd tell her just how he felt and planned to get that kiss.

Sabrina put the final touches on the birthday cake. She couldn't decide how to decorate it. Brent was so many things—a Christian, a pro-life counselor, the food pantry director. His birthday was on Valentine's Day. He enjoyed basketball and card games. He was a terrific friend, great listener, wonderful man. *And I love him.*

She bit the inside of her lip. She'd think about that later. Right now, she needed to add one more heart. Her cake design was quite intricate. A 3-D, brown-haired man sat behind a desk, holding a basketball in his hand. A car seat carrying a newborn sat on one side of the figure and a grocery bag filled with food sat on the other side. The front of the desk was decorated with chained hearts to depict the holiday. At the bottom, she'd written "Happy Birthday, Brent" in bright blue, his favorite color.

Mallory stood beside her. "Wow, sis. You did a great job. I think you'd get picked for the next great baker on *Cake Boss*."

Sabrina giggled, "So, you think Buddy would be proud?"

Her sister wrapped her arm around Sabrina's shoulder. "He'd snatch you up and make you move to New Jersey to work in his shop, and I'd never get to see you."

Sabrina rolled her eyes at her sister's dramatics. She looked at the clock. "We don't have much time. I've got to get this place decorated." She glanced at Mallory. Her sister's hands seemed swollen again. Her brow furrowed. "What's the matter?"

Mallory pressed her hand against her temple. "Just been getting some headaches lately." She glanced down at her feet, lifted one and twirled it around. "And I don't know what's up with the swelling."

"I think swelling's normal."

"This early? I'm only twenty-three weeks."

Sabrina shrugged. "I don't know. Did you call the doctor?"

"No. My appointment is next week. I'm sure it's just discomfort from the pregnancy." She chuckled, but Sabrina could tell it was forced. "Lots of women are miserable, right?"

Sabrina reached into her front pocket. She'd fix this right now. Call Dr. Coe and find out if the symptoms were unusual.

Mallory touched Sabrina's hand. "Don't worry about it. You have a party to be ready for in just over an hour."

Sabrina's stomach churned. She didn't have much time. Tab was bringing baked spaghetti and garlic bread. Lisa was bringing salad and paper products. And Laura was bringing drinks. The brownies, cream puffs, and cookies were ready, but she still had to decorate the house. She nudged Mallory toward the bedroom. "Why don't you go lie down and rest before everyone gets here?"

"I can try to help."

"No. This house is going to be hopping with eleven adults and eight kids in just over an hour—"

"Jacob's coming, too."

"Okay, make that twelve adults. You need to try to feel better."

Mallory didn't protest, and Sabrina knew her sister was feeling pretty bad. She tried not to worry as she put up streamers and blew up balloons. The last time she'd done anything like this was when Mallory was ten. She couldn't deny it was a lot of fun.

The doorbell rang, and Sabrina welcomed Lisa and Matt and their children inside the house. Before they had time to arrange the salad, Laura and Nick arrived, and then Tab and Will. Mallory came out of the bedroom, and Sabrina could tell her head still hurt. She watched as her sister went into the kitchen and took pain reliever from the cabinet. The doctor said she could take them, but Mallory still avoided medicine. *Which means she's really hurting. God, please let her be okay.*

"Bet you've never had this many people in your house, have you?" said Tab.

Sabrina shook her head, determined to focus on her friends and not worry about her sister. "Never."

But she enjoyed the company. Her house wasn't ostentatious like her parents' home, but she had plenty of room—a living room for the adults to sit in and a family room with a Playstation set up for the kids.

Her cell phone dinged, and she pulled it out of her front pocket. Jacob walked in front of her, and she bit back a laugh. She had so many people in the house, she didn't even realize he'd come in. She opened the text message then yelled, "Everyone! We have to get quiet and hide. They're almost here."

The children squealed, and parents reached for the ones who belonged to them as they tried to hide in clumps behind her couch and chairs. She hadn't seen Brent since he'd gotten his cast off. His leg was probably still a bit sensitive, and she hoped they'd didn't clobber him when he arrived.

"Remember," she said. "Wait for my signal. We don't want him to fall over from shock and end up in a cast again."

She heard a few giggles from the kids, and she was pretty sure Tab's voice was among them. The doorbell rang, and she opened it, but she didn't let him move past the foyer. Brent looked good in his khakis and blue button-down shirt. Even though most of the shirt was covered by his coat, she could tell the bright color brought out the blue in his eyes, and for a moment, she found herself lost in them.

"Hi," he said.

"Happy Birthday." She grabbed hold of his arms, and he started to lean toward her. He was going to kiss her. She knew he was. And she wanted him to. So badly. But not in front of his whole family and friends. Not the first time. Where were his parents anyway? Hiding in the car? Deciding his dad must be avoiding the noise, she snapped her fingers, and the whole crew jumped out from their hiding places. "Surprise!"

Brent took a step back, and she held his arm tightly as they walked into the living area. He looked down at her. "What is all this?"

She shrugged. "A birthday party."

"Happy Birthday, man," said Will as he grabbed him in a hug.

Sabrina stepped back and watched as the whole lot raced to him and showered him with hugs and pats and kisses on the cheek. She'd never had anything like this growing up. It had always been just her, her parents, and her sister. She had never realized how much they had missed.

She walked to her sister and wrapped her arm around Mallory's shoulder. Things would be different now they were older. Now they had Christ in their lives. Career and stature in the community weren't the most important things. Faith and family topped them.

Once his family and friends had finished wishing him a happy birthday, Sabrina walked back to him. He grabbed her hand in his and kissed her knuckles. Her knees weakened, and she sucked in her breath. "This is really nice, Sabrina."

Inwardly, she ordered her nerves to settle as she guided him into the kitchen. She pointed out the food. "Tab and your sisters made dinner, and I made your cake."

His eyes widened as he bent over to inspect her design. She wanted him to like it. She was surprised at how much she'd enjoyed putting the cake together and how much she wanted his approval. He stood up and looked at her. "Sabrina, this is amazing."

Her cheeks warmed. "Thanks."

"No, seriously. You have a lot of talent."

Mallory pointed at her. "Next great baker right here."

Sabrina nudged her sister's arm then felt Brent's arms wrap around her. She melted into his embrace, drinking in the scent of his cologne, the feel of him against her. She felt his lips pressed against her head. How she wanted to feel those lips against her own. They'd waited long enough. Each time she thought he would kiss her something happened. Temptation to look up and claim his lips herself kneaded through her. But she held back. She didn't want to kiss him in front of his whole family.

He released his embrace but kept her hand secured in his. She didn't mind. She enjoyed his touch. His dad led them in a prayer so they could eat. Sabrina and Brent waited while his sisters' and friends' families got their food. He pulled her into the hallway. Cupping her chin with his hand, he studied her face. She reminded herself to breath.

"I think this is the best birthday I've ever had."

Sabrina chuckled and lifted one eyebrow. "Better than when you were a kid?"

"Absolutely. You wanna know why?"

"Why?"

He started to lean down. This was it. He was going to kiss her. Finally. Her lips ached to be touched. "Because you're here."

He pressed his lips to her cheek then stepped back into the kitchen. Sabrina suppressed a growl. The man was never going to kiss her.

Chapter 15

Sabrina's chest tightened as she watched Dr. Coe's face contort into deep concentration. He flipped through Mallory's chart several pages. "Your blood pressure is higher than it was during the first trimester. Tell me the symptoms you're having."

Sabrina sat in the chair opposite Mallory. Her sister lifted her hand to her head. "I've been having headaches. They never completely go away. Maybe that's the blood pressure."

"Hmm. How bad? On a scale of one to ten."

Mallory wrinkled her nose. "Probably just a three right now."

Sabrina released a breath. She didn't know what the headaches could mean, but Dr. Coe seemed so serious as he jotted down everything Mallory said. Surely a headache with a rate of three wouldn't be bad.

He grabbed Mallory's hand and twisted it palm up. "Your hands are swollen. Feet, too?"

Mallory nodded.

"What about urination? Any changes?"

"I'm not going as much."

Dr. Coe frowned. "Okay. How often?"

Mallory shrugged. "I don't know. Six or seven times a day. I still get up once at night, but I figured that was normal once you get past the first trimester. Someone told me the first and third were the worst."

He nodded, seemingly pleased with her answer as he wrote on the chart. He looked at Mallory over the rims of his glasses. "That may be somewhat true, but you are pregnant. A baby sits next to your bladder. You'll still need to go frequently."

Worry wrapped around Sabrina's heart. Something was wrong. He was asking too many questions. Seemed too concerned. She rubbed her hands together. "What is it, Dr. Coe? What do you think is going on?"

Mallory pierced her with a look of anger. "Nothing's wrong. We heard the heartbeat today and everything. My baby girl's fine. Right, Dr. Coe?"

He leaned back and held the chart against his chest. "Mallory, your blood pressure is 145 over 92. That's high. Your hands and feet are swollen. You've gained five pounds in a month. Mild, consistent headaches. Less frequent urination. I believe you're in the beginning stage of preeclampsia."

Sabrina's mind started to spin. Preeclampsia? What was that? It had another name. She'd heard it before.

Dr. Coe continued, "It's also called toxemia."

That was the word she'd heard. A woman who worked for the coffee shop had it. Panic swelled inside Sabrina. The woman had lost the baby.

Sabrina stood and went to her sister. She grabbed Mallory's hand. "What does this mean? What do we do?"

"It means she has high blood pressure and protein in her urine." He jotted something on the chart again. "I'm going to have you urinate in a cup. Let us test it. Then I'll be back to talk with you some more."

Mallory followed Dr. Coe out of the office. Sabrina slid to her knees. She clasped her hands together and bowed her head. "Please, God. Please take care of Mallory and the baby. I'll do anything she needs. Just tell me and I'll do it."

"I'm in control, Sabrina," the Spirit nudged. Sabrina felt tears well in her eyes. She wanted control. She wanted to take care of things. She wanted to *know*—for God to promise—that nothing would happen to the baby.

"God, You kept her from the miscarriage. Please, God, I know You have a plan for this little girl."

"I'm in control, Sabrina."

The words came again, almost audibly in her ear. She wanted to believe them. Wanted to know that God had the best planned for Mallory and the baby. But she was scared. Losing a child had been the worst pain she'd ever endured. She didn't want Mallory to go through it. She didn't want to lose her precious niece.

The doorknob jostled, and Mallory walked back in the room. She stood and swiped her eyes with the back of her hand. She had to be strong for her sister. Couldn't show the fear she felt.

Mallory gripped Sabrina's hand. "I'm scared."

Sabrina's lower lip quivered, but she forbade any tears from falling. "Me, too."

In moments Dr. Coe returned. "Okay, Mallory. We've set up the ultrasound room. We're going to check on the baby before I let you go home."

A spark of hope ignited in Sabrina's heart. If he was talking about her going home, things might not be too bad.

She followed Mallory in the room. Her sister lay down, and the technician squirted the petroleum jelly on her stomach. Within moments, they saw the baby. Sabrina gasped. "She's so much bigger."

The baby looked healthy. Big head. Small arms and legs. She even seemed to move her legs a bit. Her hand was close to her mouth.

Mallory laughed. "Is she sucking her thumb?"

"Probably," said the technician.

Sabrina glanced up at her sister's face and brushed back strands of hair from her forehead. "She's beautiful."

The technician printed several pictures and handed them to Mallory. They made their way back to the room. Her niece looked great. She was even moving around quite a bit. Everything had to be fine. Mallory released an exhausted sigh. Sabrina couldn't blame her. They'd been here three hours. She was starving and knew Mallory had to be as well.

Dr. Coe came back into the room. He sat in front of Mallory and placed his hand on her knee. "You have pre-eclampsia. It is a very serious condition, so you have to do everything I say."

Mallory nodded. Tears welled in her eyes, and Sabrina couldn't stop the tears that filled hers as well. She grabbed her phone out of her pocket. She'd type everything he said and make sure Mallory got everything she needed.

"You're to go on complete bed rest."

Mallory gasped. "My classes?"

Dr. Coe shook his head. "You'll have to drop them. You won't be able to attend, and quite frankly, even if the college did allow you to take them online, you don't need the stress."

Sabrina sucked in her breath. She didn't want her sister to get behind in school, but they would do whatever it took to make sure Mallory and the baby were healthy.

Dr. Coe continued, "I want you to lie on your left side. All the time. When you think you can't take it anymore, I want you to lie there longer. Do you understand?"

Sabrina nodded with Mallory, even though Dr. Coe wasn't facing her.

"Eat as little salt as possible. And lastly, I'll want to see you once a week from now on." He patted her knee and smiled. "It will be the one time per week you can get up off your left side."

Sabrina closed her phone and shoved it back in her front pocket. "Will the baby be okay?"

Dr. Coe pursed his lips. "I can't promise that. You're a full twenty-four weeks. We want to get you to at least thirty-seven." He shook his head. "But if the preeclampsia worsens, I will have to take the baby. Regardless, you will have to have a cesarean."

Sabrina's brain whirled with all he'd said. Her stomach churned and her heart ached. The pain etched across Mallory's features dug into Sabrina, and she wanted to take the hurt from her sister.

"Any more questions?" asked Dr. Coe.

Mallory shook her head, and he walked out of the room. Sabrina pulled Mallory into an embrace. "We'll do everything Dr. Coe said."

Mallory nodded. "Everything."

Sabrina started to let go, but Mallory held tight. Sabrina raked her fingers through her sister's hair when she felt the warm wetness of Mallory's silent tears through the shoulder of her shirt.

"I don't want to drop my classes. I've been doing so good."

"I know."

"And I don't want a C-section." Mallory's back shook as the tears came down with more fervor.

"I know," cooed Sabrina. She held her sister, silently begging God to give Mallory peace. To give her faith.

Mallory raised her head and pulled away. She grabbed a tissue off the counter and wiped her eyes and nose. "And I wanted a hamburger."

Sabrina couldn't help but smile. "I'll go to the store and get you some turkey burgers and some fresh fruits and vegetables."

Mallory released a groan, and Sabrina looped her arm through her sister's. "Let's get you home and on your left side."

That night after purchasing every low-in-salt food she could find at the grocery, she listened from her bedroom as Mallory told Jacob about the doctor's visit. With each sniffle, Sabrina's stomach twisted. She picked up her Bible and flipped to the concordance. She was scared, so afraid for her sister. And for her precious niece. She had to be strong, but right now she felt as weak as a pot of coffee made with used grounds.

She flipped to Philippians and read that she wasn't supposed to be anxious. Not about anything. But that she was to present God with her requests, and that He would give her peace like she'd never known. She shut her eyes and whispered, "God, give Mallory strength. Keep the preeclampsia mild. Allow my niece to be born healthy."

She swallowed. "Help me trust You no matter what." The pain of the D & C all those years ago swept through her mind. Remembering the emptiness that followed, she squeezed her eyes tighter. "No matter what, help me trust You."

* * *

Brent lifted the slow cooker filled with roast beef and vegetables off the floorboard of his car. The bland dinner was not one he normally had on a date, but if he wanted to spend any time with Sabrina, it would have to do.

Four weeks had passed since they'd learned Mallory had preeclampsia. She seemed to have done well, each doctor visit ending on a positive note. However, Sabrina would only leave her sister to go to work. Even then, most days Jacob's mom agreed to stay with Mallory, he believed, more for Sabrina's peace of mind than Mallory's.

He breathed in the March air. It had been a nice day, the weather filled with promises that spring was just around the corner. He knocked on the front door, and a somber-looking Jacob answered. "Enter at your own risk."

Brent walked into the house. He could hear muffled crying coming from the living room. Praying Mallory and the baby were fine, he placed the food on the counter, plugged in the slow cooker then made his way to the living room. Mallory lay on her left side, wiping her eyes with a tissue. Sabrina sat across from her, her eyes puffy and red.

"Don't cry, Mallory. You can't upset yourself," said Sabrina.

"You're the one who made me cry," Mallory hissed. "I knew we shouldn't have told you. We should have just done it."

Brent shoved his hands in his jean pockets. "Is everything all right with the baby?"

Sabrina stood. She walked toward him and gave him a hug. "I'm sorry. I didn't hear you come in." She motioned toward Mallory. "The baby is fine, but my sister is being foolish."

Jacob sat on the floor in front of the couch where Mallory lay. He took her hand in his. "We're not being foolish. I love Mallory."

Brent's stomach knotted. Uh-oh. He had a feeling he knew where this conversation was headed. Jacob had stopped by the office and shared his plans with Brent. He knew it wasn't going to go over well with Sabrina. He looked at her. His assumption had been right.

Sabrina turned toward him. "Do you know what they want to do? They want to get married."

"You don't have a say in this, Sabrina," Mallory cried. "I'm nineteen."

Sabrina didn't look at her sister. She kept her gaze trained on him as she pointed toward the couch. "Did you hear that?"

Jacob leaned closer to Mallory and whispered in her ear. Mallory exhaled a long breath and wiped her face with the tissue again. Jacob looked at him. "It's like I told you at the center. I want my daughter to come home from the hospital to our home." He pointed from Mallory to himself. "I want to take care of my family. This wasn't the best way to start, but it's where we are, and God is big enough to get us through this."

Sabrina hadn't taken her gaze from Brent. She lifted her eyebrows. "You knew about this?"

Brent grabbed her hand. "Let's go sit on the deck."

To his surprise, she didn't argue as he led her out the back door. She flopped onto a wooden patio chair, and Brent sat down beside her. She shook her head. "I can't believe she's doing this. It's crazy. They barely know each other."

Brent nodded. "That's true, but they are seeking God, and they are having a baby together."

Sabrina leaned forward, resting her elbows on her

knees. She covered her face with her hands. "How am I supposed to protect her if she's not even in my house?"

He scooted to the edge of the chair and placed his hand on Sabrina's back. "You can't protect her from everything, Sabrina. Only God can do that."

He expected Sabrina to break down into a new tirade of tears, but she didn't. She sat still, staring at the deck. After what seemed an eternity, she looked up at him. "I've never told you about my past, and I think you need to know it."

Brent swallowed the knot in his throat. He'd known since he first met her that something had happened. She'd been pregnant. He was sure of that. Didn't know if she'd given the baby up, miscarried, or had an abortion. What if the truth was she'd had an abortion?

The thought of it turned his stomach. The videos he'd seen of procedures, the women he'd talked with who'd had them, the lives of the babies lost.

Six months ago, he'd never have considered loving a woman who'd had an abortion. He planned to love a woman like Ivy or Carrie, someone whose life wasn't tainted by "big" sins. He inwardly huffed. Sin was sin, no matter what form it took. If Sabrina's past included her having had an abortion, he would still love her. He had no doubt she was the woman God had selected to be his wife.

He nodded. "Okay. Tell me."

"When I was Mallory's age I got pregnant." She stopped and looked at him, her gaze searching his reaction—if he condemned or accepted her.

He nodded again. "I had already figured that out."

She squinted. "How?"

"At the hospital when you were afraid Mallory was miscarrying. You said, 'not her, too.' "

She pointed to her chest. "Well, I did miscarry." Tears welled in her eyes, and he took her hand in his. She pulled away and swiped at her eyes with the back of her hand. "You have to know the truth, though. I was going to abort the baby. My parents said I had to, and I was scheduled for the procedure." She shook her head. "And I know I would have done it."

Brent stood and pulled her into his arms. "Sabrina, I'm sorry."

She wrapped her arms around him, and he held her tight, raking his fingers through her hair. Though he didn't want to, he pulled away to arm's length. Gazing into her deep brown eyes, he saw vulnerability and fear. "It's in the past. No matter what you would have done. It's in the past, and you're a new creation. It's forgiven." She blinked, and he knew she still waged an inner war to forgive herself. "And I love you."

Her eyes widened. He couldn't take it anymore. Wasn't going to wait another moment. He leaned toward her and claimed her lips with his. Their sweet softness drew him, and he pulled her closer. She responded, tracing her fingertips up his neck until she gripped his hair. He deepened the kiss, allowing her sweetness to course through him until he knew he had to pull away while he still had the strength.

He stepped back and sucked in his breath. She touched her fingertips to her lips, a look of longing gleaming from her eyes. She shook her head. "No."

He frowned, but before he could ask what she meant, she covered the distance between them, grabbed his shirt, and planted her lips against his again. Trying to keep his wits about him, he kept his arms at his sides, balling his fists. Her lips tasted like heaven, and he found himself getting lost in their sweetness. Conjuring up the last of his willpower, he pulled away again. "Sabrina."

She laughed and placed her finger against her lips again. "Do you know how long I have waited for you to do that?"

He tried to calm his racing heart. "A long time."

She stepped toward him again and placed a quick kiss on his lips. He lifted his hands. "Seriously, woman. You're killing me."

Her expression grew serious. "You said you loved me."

He lowered his hands. "I do."

"I love you, too."

Thanksgiving filled his heart. He'd prayed for her salvation, knowing that if she never received Christ, he could never pursue her. Not only did she become a Christian but she fell in love with him as well. *God, You are too good to me.*

He drew her closer again. "Do you know how long I've waited to hear those words?"

"Is it as long as I've waited for that kiss?"

Brent laughed. "I think I fell in love with you the first time you walked through my office door."

She lifted her eyebrows. "Seriously?"

"Yeah. Waiting on you has definitely taught me a thing or two about patience."

"Well, I still haven't learned it." A look of mischief crossed her face. "So, can I have another kiss?"

"I think I can do that."

He lowered his head and claimed her lips with his once more. The past was over. It was time to begin their future. Together.

Chapter 16

Sabrina opened the front door and stepped outside to join Brent on the sidewalk. The sun shone bright, and the air had grown warmer through April. "She's made it to thirty-three weeks."

Brent pressed a quick kiss to her lips. "I know. Are you going to let me take you out for dinner, or do I need to go pick something up and bring it back?"

Sabrina grabbed Brent's hand. She loved this man. He never complained that she didn't want to go on real dates, that she wanted to stay home with her sister. Which was the reason Mallory and Jacob made her promise she'd go to dinner with him tonight. She smiled. "Nope. We're going out."

"All right." He grinned and pumped his fist through the air. Placing his hand in the small of her back, he guided her to his car.

"I do want to do something first."

"No problem."

"I want you to meet my parents."

Brent turned in the seat and faced her. Confusion etched his features, but he didn't look as if he would refuse. "Are you ready for that?"

She nodded. "I want them to meet you." She patted on the top of her purse. "And I have an ultrasound picture with me. They need to know Mallory and Jacob are getting married next week. Even though it's going to be just a small ceremony at my house."

"All right. Tell me where I'm going."

She told him the directions. Inwardly, she prayed her parents would be receptive to their visit. For all she knew, they wouldn't be home. But if they were, she wanted them to be nice to Brent. Though Mallory didn't say it, Sabrina knew her sister wanted them to be at the wedding next week.

She rested her hand on Brent's elbow. "There is no telling what they may say."

"I'm a big boy. I can handle it."

He pulled into the driveway, and she fought the urge to tell him to pull out and head to the restaurant. Brent got out of the car, walked around, and opened her door. She held his hand as they made their way up the sidewalk. She pressed the doorbell and waited. Her mother opened the door, dressed to the nines in black slacks and a hot pink blouse. To Sabrina's surprise, she smiled and opened the door wider. "Hello, Sabrina. Come on in."

They walked inside, and Sabrina took in the familiar marble floors and pillars that reached from the second floor down. All around them shone bright white walls and furnishings and mahogany trimmings. It was immaculately decorated. Pristine and clean. Cold and unforgiving. Glancing at Brent, pride swelled within her. He wasn't fazed by her parents' wealth. He looked at her mom. "You have a lovely home, Mrs. Moore."

"Thank you, young man." Her mother cocked her head. "Sabrina, won't you introduce me to your friend?"

"This is Brent Connors, my boyfriend."

Brent extended his hand, and her mother shook it.

"Mitch told me he thought you might have your eye set on someone else." Her father's voice boomed as he walked into the foyer. "Must say, he was mighty disappointed."

Sabrina sucked in her breath, and heat warmed her cheeks. Her father couldn't possibly be any ruder. She grabbed Brent's hand, ready to turn around and get out of there. He squeezed her hand, and she knew he didn't want her to bolt. He extended his free hand to her father. "Hello, Mr. Moore."

Her father shook his hand then motioned for them to follow him into the parlor. She sat with Brent on the couch, and her parents sat in wingback chairs across from them. Her father leaned forward in the chair, placed his elbows on his knees, and clapped his hands. "So, tell us about yourself. Brent, did you say? What do you do for a living?"

Sabrina straightened her shoulders. This was going to be bad. Really bad. She looked at Brent. He wasn't intimidated or upset, and she found herself loving him all the more. "I'm a counselor."

Her mother lifted her eyebrows and nodded to her father. "Really? Wonderful employment. Where do you work?"

"I'm a counselor at the ProLife Pregnancy Center in town. It's where I met your daughters."

Sabrina sucked in her breath as her mother bristled and her father hopped out of his chair and stalked out of the room. Brent's countenance remained unchanged as he turned his attention to her mother. "Sabrina wanted to come today to let you know that Mallory is getting married next week."

Her mother gasped. "What?"

Sabrina lifted her chin, drawing strength from Brent. She pulled the ultrasound picture from her purse and handed it to her mother. "Next Saturday at two o'clock at my house. Come if you'd like. Mallory's been on bed rest with preeclampsia, but this is a picture of your granddaughter. She is perfect."

Her mother's face reddened, and Sabrina didn't wait for her retort. She squeezed Brent's hand, and they stood and walked out of the house. Once in the car, she blew out a breath. "We did it." She turned to Brent and smiled. "You were wonderful. It actually wasn't as bad as I feared."

Brent raised one eyebrow. "Was Mitch the doctor you went out with?"

Sabrina cringed. In her nervousness about inviting them to the wedding, she'd forgotten her father's unkind comment. "Yeah."

Brent pulled out of the driveway. "Can't say that I blame the guy for being disappointed."

Sabrina pressed her head against the seat and laughed. "Does that mean you're glad I picked you?"

He lifted her hand to his lips and kissed her knuckles. "Definitely what I mean."

She sobered when she looked out the window as they passed through her parents' neighborhood. Some of the wealthiest people in Tennessee lived in this gated community. Growing up, she assumed she would live in a house as elaborate as the one she'd been raised in. Now, she didn't care about the size of the house. Instead, she wanted her home to be filled with love and family. Her stomach still felt queasy from the visit. She glanced at Brent. "I don't think I'm ready to eat yet."

"You want me to take you where I go when I'm stressed?"

"Sure."

Brent drove into a poorer section of town. Sabrina had never been to this area, and she didn't know what to make of the small houses with tattered roofs and shutters. The vinyl fell from the sides of some of them, along with wooden boards covering a few of the windows. He pulled into a small lot alongside a concrete building with a wooden sign on the front that read, "Food Pantry."

She looked at Brent, guilt niggled her heart. "I can't believe I've known you all this time and I've never been here."

"You have been busy taking care of your sister."

She nodded, but his comment didn't make her feel any better. She'd lived most of her life in Greenfield, and she'd never seen the place that was a crucial means of food for several in her community. *And my mother was a state representative. One who bragged about her efforts to help the poor.*

He unlocked the door, and she followed him inside. She took in the metal shelves that reached all the way to the ceiling and formed smaller versions of the aisles she perused in the grocery store. Labels hung from the ceiling, marking where to find cereal, canned vegetables, fruits, and meats. Large, mismatched refrigerators lined the wall closest to the door.

She remembered the unused but still working refrigerator that sat in her family's basement when she was a child. It hadn't matched her mother's new appliances, so she'd put it in the basement. Why didn't her parents give it away to someone who needed one? Or to the food pantry?

"Come on." Brent motioned for her to follow him to the back of the building. Grocery bags filled with cans sat on the floor. He pointed to them. "When I'm stressed, I organize the donations."

He picked up a bag and walked toward the aisles. Pulling out a can of beans, he pointed to the labels hanging from the ceiling. He walked down aisle three and placed the beans with several cans like it. "Just put them where they go."

Sabrina picked up a bag and started putting the foods in the places they belonged. *God, I have so much, and there are many people with so little. Teach me to be aware of others' needs. Not just my family.*

With the last bag emptied, Sabrina wrapped her arms around Brent. He chuckled as he returned her hug. "What's this for?" He kissed the top of her head. "Not that I mind, but—"

"I'm just so thankful I met you. You helped introduce me to the Lord. You've counseled my sister. Welcomed me into your family." She opened her arms and turned around the room. "Showed me a world I didn't know."

He pulled her back into his embrace. "You forgot to mention that I love you."

"And you love me." Her stomach growled, and she smacked it with both hands. "And apparently, you need to feed me."

Brent laughed, and they walked back to the car. This had been the best date she'd ever had.

Brent adjusted his tie as he walked into Sabrina's living room. Earlier that day, he and Jacob had cleared the furniture out of the room and set up a few rows of wooden chairs. Sabrina tied lavender bows around the chairs. She'd also rented an arch to sit in front of the large window and purchased two flower arrangements to sit on each side. He knew the decorations weren't what Sabrina would have wanted for Mallory, but they were still nice.

"We need to hurry up and do this. She needs to get back on her left side."

Brent turned at the sound of Sabrina's voice. She looked beautiful with lavender flowers in her hair and wearing a purple dress that hugged her waist then flared at her knees. He placed a quick kiss on her lips. "It will be fine, and you are beautiful."

Sabrina released a sigh. "I'm so nervous."

He cupped her chin with his hand. "Enjoy this time with your sister."

She nodded, and within moments Jacob's dad and brothers arrived as well as a few of Mallory's and Jacob's friends. Jacob's mother had spent the day with Mallory and Sabrina, helping with hair and makeup. Sabrina had fussed that she would have wanted Mallory to have a day at the salon. Brent had tried to assure her Mallory would be fine without one. She hadn't seemed thrilled with his response, but he didn't know what else to say.

Brent guided the guests to their seats. He noticed Sabrina glanced at the door several times. He knew she watched to see if her parents would arrive. When time for the ceremony arrived, they still hadn't shown. Frustration swelled within him. He knew they weren't coming. He bit back the anger he felt. They had to know their daughters would want them here. *God, forgive them. And help me to forgive them, too.*

The pastor and Jacob stood beneath the arch. One of Jacob's friends stood beside them. Sabrina had talked them into renting tuxes, even though Jacob thought it wasn't necessary. Brent didn't really understand the big deal about it, either, but women thought differently.

Music started to play from a stereo, and Brent took his

seat. Sabrina and Mallory walked down the short aisle. Despite her pregnant belly, Mallory seemed to glow in the cream-colored, lace-covered gown Jacob's mother had sewn. Brent couldn't believe how pretty she looked. Young but happy. He glanced toward Jacob. The young man's smile couldn't have gotten any wider. Brent knew God would see her and Jacob through their upcoming challenges, if they relied on Him.

Brent tried to listen to the ceremony, but he couldn't take his eyes off Sabrina. He wanted to make her his wife. He wanted to promise to have and to hold her forever. Until death parted them.

Jacob and Mallory said their "I dos," and they kissed. Their first kiss as husband and wife. Brent watched the emotions that played on Sabrina's face. She wanted to be happy for her sister. He knew she tried. But Sabrina hadn't completely let go of her need to protect and control. He couldn't completely blame her. He'd have a hard time if the situation were reversed and it was one of his sisters.

The pastor invited everyone to stay for cake, and Sabrina hurried Mallory and Jacob through sharing the first piece. The ceremony started at two, and within forty-five minutes, Jacob was loading Mallory into his car to take her back to their apartment so she could lie down. Not the kind of honeymoon Brent hoped for. He sent up a silent prayer asking God to allow them a honeymoon in the future.

Soon after, the guests left.

Brent made his way to Sabrina. Her face was downcast, and he knew her first night without her sister would be difficult. He wished he could stay with her, comfort her, but he knew nothing godly would come from it. *Soon enough, Lord, I will make her mine. Give me patience.*

He traced her cheek with the back of his hand, thankful the sun shone and the temperature was warm. A perfect day for what he had planned. "Let's get out of here."

Sabrina's gaze flitted around the room. "There's no way. I've got to clean up this mess."

"I'll take care of that. Go put on some old clothes. I want to take you somewhere."

She placed her hands on her hips. "There is no way you can clean up this whole place while I change clothes. I am not going anywhere."

His cell phone dinged, and he looked at the text. Grinning, he opened the front door to let his sisters inside. "I'm not going to clean it. They are."

Laura laughed as she pushed a strand of hair behind her ear. "He's paying us the big bucks, too. So whatever you have planned, go have fun."

Lisa frowned. "He's paying you?"

Laura pushed Lisa's arm. "I was kidding."

Brent shook his head at his sisters. He turned back to Sabrina. "See. It's all taken care of. Go put on some old clothes."

Sabrina sighed. "All right." She looked at Laura and Lisa. "Thanks so much. I feel like I'm about to melt into a pile of mush."

While she changed clothes, Brent grabbed his bib overalls and a T-shirt from the back seat of his car, went back into the house, and changed. He walked out of the bathroom, and Laura lifted one eyebrow. "Are you sure you wanna do this with her?"

"Yep."

Lisa scrunched her nose. "It's not what I'd want to do." She nodded to the chairs they'd started stacking. "I'd rather deal with this."

Sabrina came out of her bedroom in a pretty green jumpsuit, and he pointed for her to go back and pick something older. He could tell she bit back a laugh at his attire, but she changed again into something more appropriate.

Once they got in the car, Sabrina turned to him. "Where are we going?"

"It's a surprise."

Brent drove the country road leading to his parents' house. He knew they wouldn't be home, out flea marketing for the day. He also knew Sabrina had probably never done what he had planned, but by the end of the day she'd be so sore and tired, she wouldn't be able to fret over Mallory.

Once he pulled into the driveway, Sabrina frowned. "What are we doing here?"

He grinned. "We're going to get the place ready for spring. Pull weeds. Spread a little mulch. Till the garden."

Sabrina raised one eyebrow. "What?"

He hopped out and ran around and opened her door. "Come on. It'll be fun."

She stumbled out of the car. "I've never done any of those things."

"First time for everything."

He grabbed her hand and guided her to the shed. After handing her a pair of his mother's work gloves, he put on a pair of his own. They walked to the front yard, and he showed her how to pull weeds around the bushes. Once she could distinguish the weeds from the future flowers, he took the clippers and trimmed the shrubs. They shoved the weeds and clippings into garbage bags; then he poured mulch while she raked it evenly.

She stood, placed her hand on her back, and stretched. "I'm so sore."

He lifted his eyebrows. "What? We haven't even made it to the backyard."

She moaned and grabbed her stomach. "Can you at least feed me first?"

"Yep." He walked into the house and grabbed the cooler he'd already prepared. Taking it outside, he set it on the patio table. "I've got the deli sandwiches all ready."

Without commenting, Sabrina grabbed her sandwich and gobbled the whole thing. Her hair stuck to her forehead and cheeks in chunks, and streams of dirt traveled down her face from where she'd sweated. And yet, she was still the prettiest woman he'd ever seen.

She swallowed down a bottle of water, and Brent had a niggling of guilt that he'd worked her too hard. He knew she'd never done anything like this and would probably be sore for a few days afterward.

She let out a quick breath. "So, what's next?"

Brent showed her what to pull around his mother's back-yard flower gardens. He got out the tiller and prepared the vegetable garden for planting. By the time he finished, she had already poured mulch and was raking it out. The sun was beginning to set, and it was time to call it quits.

He put the tiller back in the shed then walked behind Sabrina and wrapped his arms around her. "You did a great job today."

She leaned the back of her head against his chest. "I can't believe you made me do all this work. I've never been so tired in my life."

Brent grinned. "But I bet you'll sleep tonight."

Sabrina turned around and looked up at him. "You did this so I wouldn't fret about Mallory."

He wrinkled his nose and lifted his hands. "Guilty."

"You're a smart guy."

He chuckled. "Guilty, again." He wrapped his arms around her and rested his chin on the top of her head.

She pressed her cheek against his chest. "I actually had a lot of fun."

"I'm glad. I enjoyed having you work with me." *Soon, God, working together will be part of our daily routine.*

Chapter 17

Sabrina lifted her cell phone to her ear. "Hello."

Jacob's voice sounded over the line. "Her water broke. Meet us at the hospital."

The phone clicked off, and Sabrina gripped the phone tighter. "What?" She scooped her purse from behind the office door, pulled the phone from her ear, and tried to call Jacob's number. He didn't answer. Shoving it into her pocket, she raced toward her car. "Thirty-six weeks. That's long enough, right, Lord?"

Her heartbeat raced, and her hands shook as she sped to the hospital. Finding a parking place was a nightmare. She contemplated parking illegally, when a car pulled out of a spot near the front. She ran into the hospital and up to the second floor. Worry started to gnaw away at her. It wasn't good that Mallory's water broke. Her heartbeat raced. The cesarean was scheduled for the next week. Her hands began to feel clammy. With Mallory's water breaking, they would have to perform the C-section as an emergency. Her knees felt weak. Bad things happened in emergency situations.

She stopped. Her thoughts weren't doing her any good, and they wouldn't help Mallory. Slipping onto a chair, she leaned forward and closed her eyes. *God, You already know all of this. You've gotten her this far. She's in Your hands. Keep her and the baby safe. Give me peace, God. Peace like I've never known.*

Standing, she balled her fists and blew out a long breath. She walked to the receptionist. "I'm looking for Mallory Moore." She shook her head. "I mean Mallory Wiley."

"She's already in surgery. Won't be long now." The young blond-haired woman smiled, her expression filled with compassion and kindness. Her countenance encouraged Sabrina to stay calm, and she lifted a quick prayer of thanks for the woman's demeanor.

"Thanks. Where can I wait?"

She pointed to her left. "The waiting room is the second door on the left."

Sabrina nodded as she made her way to the room. She'd wanted to be with Mallory, to hold her hand and tell her that everything would be all right. And that had been the plan if Mallory's body had waited for the scheduled appointment next week. But this was an emergency. And Dr. Coe had told them only her husband could be with her in an emergency. And sometimes even he couldn't go.

She bit back a sigh of disbelief. Her husband? She still couldn't believe her baby sister was married. *And about to have a baby.*

She walked into the waiting room and saw Jacob's parents and his two little brothers. Relief swept through her that Jacob wasn't with them. *He must have been able to go with her to surgery.* That was a good thing. She needed to focus on the good things.

The boys sat in chairs beside each other, their gazes locked on their handheld video games. Jacob's parents stood by the window, his dad's hand draped over his mom's shoulder. She waved at them and realized she hadn't told Brent about the baby. She pulled her cell phone out of her pocket. No service.

Growling, she walked into the hall. Still no service. She traipsed a little way down the hall until she found a corner that allowed her a few bars. She tried to call, but he didn't answer. She looked at the time. Still pretty early in the day. He probably had a client. She texted him a message to meet her at the hospital then headed back to the waiting room.

An hour passed before Jacob finally walked through the waiting room door, clad in a blue hospital getup. Sabrina thought her heart might explode when she noted the full smile that spread his lips. "Five pounds, three ounces. Eighteen inches long. She and Mallory are doing great."

Tears filled Sabrina's eyes as she watched his parents and brothers rush and hug him. *Thank You, God. Thank You. Thank You. Thank You.*

Jacob nodded toward her. "Mallory wants to see you."

Her knees felt weak, and her stomach churned, but she'd do anything for her sister. Whatever she needed. With her fingertips, Sabrina pressed back the tears from the corners of her eyes and sniffed. "Is it okay? Will they let me?"

"Dr. Coe said it was fine."

Sabrina followed Jacob through the double doors. A nurse handed her a getup that matched Jacob's. After putting it on, she wiped her eyes with a tissue and washed her hands. Excitement nearly swallowed her as she walked into Mallory's room.

She bit back the tears again when she saw her sister, her hair pulled back in a messy knot, her face shining with pride and joy. In her arms was the bundle Sabrina had prayed for constantly. Moving toward her, Sabrina wrung her hands together. The small baby had a head full of dark hair, just like Mallory's and Sabrina's. She lifted her tiny hand and flexed, showing her five adorable fingers. Sabrina chewed the inside of her lip. "Oh, Mallory, she's beautiful. Absolutely perfect."

Mallory smiled up at her, tears glistened in her eyes. "You wanna know her name?"

Sabrina nodded.

"Sabrina Joy."

Sabrina cupped her hand over her mouth. For years, she'd mourned the child she lost. The child whose life she probably would have taken herself had not Sabrina's body intervened. When Mallory discovered her pregnancy, all Sabrina could think about was what she could do to protect Mallory's baby. How she could help her sister. She didn't want Mallory to endure the pain she had experienced. She learned soon enough that God was in control of what happened, and He was the one who allowed this sweet baby to be born to her sister and Jacob.

Hesitantly, she reached out and touched the child's soft hair. "You're naming her after me?"

"You've loved her with more passion than even I could conjure at times."

Sabrina released part of a laugh and sniffed back her tears.

Mallory smiled. "It seems only right to name her after you."

A nurse walked into the room. "I'm sorry, honey." She pointed to Mallory and the baby—her namesake, precious Sabrina Joy. "I need to get these two girls cleaned up and checked out."

Sabrina didn't argue. They could do whatever they needed to do to be sure her sister and niece were well taken care of. Her mind spun with happiness and thanks-giving, and she felt as if she walked on clouds as she made her way back to the waiting room.

She spied Brent and sucked in her breath. She raced to him and wrapped him in a hug. "They're fine. Wonderful. Perfect. Beautiful."

He kissed the top of her head. "I'm so glad."

"And they named her Sabrina Joy. After me. I can't—"

She looked over his shoulder and gasped. Her parents stood several feet behind them. Her mother held a vase filled with pink, yellow, and purple flowers. Sabrina released Brent and walked to them. "You came?"

Her father cleared his throat. He pointed to Brent. "Your boyfriend showed up at the house."

Her mother bit her bottom lip, uncertainty etched her brow. "He thought we might want to come."

She looked back at Brent. He grinned, and she thought her heart might burst. How she loved this man! She turned back to her parents. "Mallory will be so glad you're here."

Brent rushed to the florist shop to pick up the roses he'd ordered. He still couldn't believe Sabrina's parents had actually gone to the hospital. The idea to tell them about the baby had just been a soft prompting of the Spirit. He'd thought they'd laugh at him or shut the door in his face, but they hadn't. *Which is why I'm glad I listened to Your quiet prompting, Lord.*

After hustling in the shop, he rang the bell at the counter, and a teenage boy stepped out from the back. Brent took his wallet out of his back pocket. "Brent Connors. I ordered roses."

The boy shook his head. "That's a lot of roses, mister. She must be one special lady."

Brent grinned. "She is."

He hefted the vase that contained fifty-six red roses to his car then went back inside and picked up the box that held three dozen more. Looking at his cell phone, his heartbeat sped up. He only had thirty minutes before Jacob was supposed to send Sabrina back to her house to pick up Mallory's pink slippers. The ones she'd *accidentally* left at Sabrina's house.

He shook his head. The day wasn't supposed to go like this. They never planned for Mallory to go into labor. But things often veered from what was planned, and he'd just have to go with the flow. *You're working it out anyway, aren't You, Lord?* He pulled Sabrina's house key out of his front jean's pocket. "It's nice to be on good terms with the future sister- and brother-in-law."

He drove back to her house and took the flowers inside. He set the vase on the kitchen table. Patting his front pocket, he smiled at the feel of the little black box. Racing back to his car, he opened the container of roses and began ripping off the petals. He scattered them all the way up the sidewalk, in front of the door, and on the hardwood foyer and hall leading to the kitchen.

Releasing a sigh, he pulled out his phone and texted Jacob. "Ready."

His phone dinged, and he read Jacob's message back. "Already on her way."

His heart beat faster, and his stomach knotted. A cold sweat broke out on his forehead. He grabbed a paper towel off the dispenser, ran cold water on it then wiped his face. *Calm down, man. You can do this.*

He wanted to do this. He'd been waiting since the day she walked into the office to be able to ask her to be his wife. Still, his nerves were getting the best of him.

The front door jiggled, and he tossed the paper towel into the sink. Wiping his hands on the front of his jeans, he straightened his shoulders. Sabrina's heels clicked against the hardwood floor until she walked into the kitchen. Her face was radiant with a smile that made her eyes twinkle. She bit her bottom lip. "What's all this?"

He didn't wait. He couldn't. Covering the distance between them, he grabbed her hand in his and lowered to one knee. Her reached into his front pocket and pulled out the box. Sabrina's legs started to shake, and she continued to bite her bottom lip. Excitement shone in her deep brown eyes. "Sabrina, I love you. I—"

She shook her free hand. "Okay. Yes."

He furrowed his brow. "You didn't let me finish."

She wrinkled her nose. "Sorry. Go ahead."

He laughed and shook his head. He opened the box holding the one carat, heirloom halo diamond. "Sabrina, will you marry me?"

"I already said yes." She pointed to the ring and grinned. "And now I definitely say yes."

He laughed, stood up, and wrapped his arms around her. Releasing her just a bit, he lowered his lips to hers. For as long as he lived, he would never tire of her kiss.

"I love the rose petals leading to my house," she said.

"Pretty clever, aren't I?"

She touched one of the roses in the vase. "These are beautiful, and there are so many."

"Fifty-six. One for each day since our first kiss."

Sabrina looked up him and pressed her hand against her chest. "That is so sweet."

He shrugged. "I thought about getting one fake rose and telling you I'd love you until the last rose died, but I didn't want to be too big of a sap."

Sabrina chuckled as she lifted her hands and traced them through his hair. His blood coursed through his veins like fire. "I happen to like sappy."

"Then I'll get you a fake rose."

She shook her head. "No need. You can just keep buying more."

He laughed as he took her hand in his. "Let's go get some dinner."

She puckered. "You don't want a kiss."

"Yeah, I do. And that's the problem. It'd be best if we get out of here."

She grinned. "Let me get Mallory's slippers."

"She doesn't need them."

Sabrina's jaw dropped; then she clamped it shut. She looped her arm through his as they walked toward the door. "You really are clever."

Epilogue

Pride swelled in Sabrina's heart as she watched Jacob and then Mallory cross the stage to receive their college diplomas. She turned and looked at seven-year-old Sabrina Joy. The girl's parents had to work doubly hard to keep Christ the focus of their marriage and family. Some semesters they'd only been able to handle going to school part-time. But they'd persevered, and God had blessed them. And in a few weeks, Sabrina Joy would have a baby sister.

Micah started to fuss, and Sabrina looked at her mother. "You want me to take him?"

She nodded and handed over their only grandson.

Brent leaned over and whispered, "I'll take him so you can watch the ceremony."

Before she could respond, he scooped Micah out of her arms and headed to the back of the convention center. Looking behind her, she felt thankful that Brent was such a good dad, especially since six-month-old Micah had been such a fussy baby.

Peeking again at her parents, she saw that her four-year-old daughter, Maggie, sat in her grandpa's lap. She had her thumb in her mouth and her free hand scooped around Sabrina's dad's neck so she could twirl her fingers around his hair. If anyone could soften her father's heart toward Christ, it would be that child. From the moment she was born, Maggie hadn't been dissuaded by his gruffness. She loved her grandpa, and Sabrina had watched as his hardened heart had started to melt.

Sabrina turned her attention back to the stage. The president of the university gave his final words and the ceremony ended. Sabrina and her family and Jacob's family waited in the lobby until Jacob and Mallory made their way to them.

While Jacob hugged his parents and brothers, Sabrina grabbed Mallory in an embrace. "You did it."

"By God's grace, we did." Mallory wrapped her arm around Sabrina Joy.

The child smiled up at her mother. "I'm proud of you, Mommy."

Contentment filled Sabrina as she watched her sister bend down and kiss the child's cheek. She stood up. "Now as soon as this little one's born"—she pointed to her belly—"I'll be able to start working at the hospital."

"Nursing is hard work," said her mother. "You might want to start out part-time."

Sabrina grinned, as she watched Mallory try not to roll her eyes. Their mother hadn't known a day of hard, physical work in her life. And when she'd been Mallory's age, she'd been determined to conquer the world. Wasn't the least bit worried about resting up or spending time with her family. And yet, their mother had been involved since Sabrina Joy's birth. Most of the time, anyway. They both still prayed for their parents' salvation. Becoming grand-parents had softened their hearts.

Sabrina nudged her sister's arm. "Mom makes a good point."

Mallory sighed. "I know. Jacob doesn't want me to try to work full-time."

Sabrina bit her lip. She knew Jacob would probably have to tie her sister down. She enjoyed helping people and hoped to work in the obstetrical unit one day. The woman struggled with the same driven-to-succeed tendencies Sabrina knew all too well. But God had tempered her, and Sabrina had learned her real success came in her relationship with Him, her family, and the people He brought in her path.

"Did Jacob get the job?" asked their dad.

Mallory nodded. "Starts teaching tenth grade biology in the fall. And he'll get to be an assistant coach for the wrestling team."

Brent walked up to them. Micah was still fussing. She hugged her sister and the rest of the family. "We better go. My little guy needs his nap."

"I wanna go with Grandpa," said Maggie.

Sabrina's dad grinned. "We were going to treat you all to dinner. If you need to take Micah home, let her tag along with us. Grandma and I will bring her home later."

Brent grinned, and she knew he hoped for a bit of alone time. She wouldn't mind some herself. He kissed Maggie's head. "Be good for your grandparents."

Just as they hoped, Micah fell asleep on the way home. Brent carried him into the house and laid him in the crib. Brent smiled at Sabrina, and she lifted her finger. "Just let me put the finishing touches on the cake for Allie's eigh-teenth birthday."

She couldn't wait for the get-together with his family the following day. The oldest grandchild was turning eighteen, graduating, and soon heading off to college. So much had changed since she'd met the Connors family. They'd taught her what a family should be like, and she never tired of getting together with them.

It had been five years since she quit her job and started decorating cakes from their home. When she'd discovered she was pregnant with Maggie, she knew she couldn't stand punching numbers and working projections for the rest of her life. She'd worked awhile behind the counter with Gretchen. But when her friend retired for good, Sabrina found she didn't want to work at the coffee shop anymore, either.

Brent wrapped his arms around her from behind. "She's going to love the cake."

Sabrina looked at the chocolate cake wrapped in bright pink fondant. She'd cut letters out of lime green fondant and written Allie's name in big letters across the length of the cake. Then she'd sculpted pink and green swirls that stuck up around the edges. "I hope so."

Brent turned her around to face him. "It seems surreal to me that my niece will be eighteen."

"It seems surreal to me that my sister just graduated college."

Brent reached up and brushed stray strands of hair behind her ear. Pleasure coursed through her. His touch still made her shiver. He traced her cheek with the back of his hand. "It seems surreal to me that you've been my wife for seven years."

Seven years. So much had changed in her life from who she was a decade ago. At that time, she was bitter, angry, hurting over her past. She had wanted to make the most of her career and find a man who wanted success more than anything else.

Then God changed Mallory. Allowed her little sister to get pregnant. Sabrina met Brent, a man who loved God with his whole being. And God wooed her to Himself. Her priorities shifted, and she learned to love, to hope, to trust.

Inhaling a deep breath, she pressed her cheek against Brent's chest. She loved to hear the steady beat of his heart. "It does seem surreal. Not a moment goes by that I'm not thankful."

He cupped her chin in his hand and lifted her face until she gazed into his clear blue eyes. "I love you, Sabrina."

"And I love you."

He lowered his lips to hers, and Sabrina accepted his kiss. His touch never failed to warm her from the inside out. He bent down and scooped her into his arms. As he walked down the hallway, she spied a picture of Sabrina Joy. Her precious niece. The child God used as a catalyst to begin Sabrina's journey to finding Him. Since then, she couldn't begin to count her blessings. There were too many to name. And they'd started with that precious baby.

* * * * *

HEARTSONG
PRESENTS

Look out for 4 new
Heartsong Presents books next month!

**Every month 4 inspiring faith-filled
romances will be available in stores.**

These contemporary and historical Christian
romances emphasize God's role in every
relationship and reinforce the importance of
faith, hope and love.

REQUEST YOUR FREE BOOKS!

2 FREE CHRISTIAN NOVELS
PLUS 2
FREE
MYSTERY GIFTS

HEARTSONG
PRESENTS

YES! Please send me 2 Free Heartsong Presents novels and my 2 FREE mystery gifts (gifts are worth about $10). After receiving them, if I don't wish to receive any more books I can return the shipping statement marked "cancel." If I don't cancel, I will receive 4 brand-new novels every month and be billed just $4.24 per book. That's a savings of 20% off the cover price. It's quite a bargain! Shipping and handling is just 50¢ per book in the U.S.* I understand that accepting the 2 free books and gifts places me under no obligation to buy anything. I can always return a shipment and cancel at any time. Even if I never buy another book, the two free books and gifts are mine to keep forever.

159 HDN FVYK

Name	(PLEASE PRINT)
Address	Apt. #
City	State	Zip

Signature (if under 18, a parent or guardian must sign)

Mail to the **Harlequin® Reader Service:**
IN U.S.A.: P.O. Box 1867, Buffalo, NY 14240-1867

* Terms and prices subject to change without notice. Prices do not include applicable taxes. Sales tax applicable in N.Y. This offer is limited to one order per household. Not valid for current subscribers to Heartsong Presents books. All orders subject to credit approval. Credit or debit balances in a customer's account(s) may be offset by any other outstanding balance owed by or to the customer. Please allow 4 to 6 weeks for delivery. Offer available while quantities last. Offer valid only in the U.S.

Your Privacy—The Harlequin® Reader Service is committed to protecting your privacy. Our Privacy Policy is available online at www.ReaderService.com or upon request from the Harlequin Reader Service.
We make a portion of our mailing list available to reputable third parties that offer products we believe may interest you. If you prefer that we not exchange your name with third parties, or if you wish to clarify or modify your communication preferences, please visit us at www.ReaderService.com/consumerchoice or write to us at Harlequin Reader Service Preference Service, P.O. Box 9062, Buffalo, NY 14269. Include your complete name and address.

HSPDIR13

REQUEST YOUR FREE BOOKS!

2 FREE INSPIRATIONAL NOVELS
PLUS 2
FREE
MYSTERY GIFTS

Love Inspired

YES! Please send me 2 FREE Love Inspired® novels and my 2 FREE mystery gifts (gifts are worth about $10). After receiving them, if I don't wish to receive any more books, I can return the shipping statement marked "cancel." If I don't cancel, I will receive 6 brand-new novels every month and be billed just $4.49 per book in the U.S. or $4.99 per book in Canada. That's a savings of at least 22% off the cover price. It's quite a bargain! Shipping and handling is just 50¢ per book in the U.S. and 75¢ per book in Canada.* I understand that accepting the 2 free books and gifts places me under no obligation to buy anything. I can always return a shipment and cancel at any time. Even if I never buy another book, the two free books and gifts are mine to keep forever.   105/305 IDN FVYV

Name	(PLEASE PRINT)

Address   Apt. #

City   State/Prov.   Zip/Postal Code

Signature (if under 18, a parent or guardian must sign)

Mail to the Harlequin® Reader Service:
IN U.S.A.: P.O. Box 1867, Buffalo, NY 14240-1867
IN CANADA: P.O. Box 609, Fort Erie, Ontario L2A 5X3

**Are you a subscriber to Love Inspired books
and want to receive the larger-print edition?
Call 1-800-873-8635 or visit www.ReaderService.com.**

* Terms and prices subject to change without notice. Prices do not include applicable taxes. Sales tax applicable in N.Y. Canadian residents will be charged applicable taxes. Offer not valid in Quebec. This offer is limited to one order per household. Not valid for current subscribers to Love Inspired books. All orders subject to credit approval. Credit or debit balances in a customer's account(s) may be offset by any other outstanding balance owed by or to the customer. Please allow 4 to 6 weeks for delivery. Offer available while quantities last.

Your Privacy—The Harlequin® Reader Service is committed to protecting your privacy. Our Privacy Policy is available online at www.ReaderService.com or upon request from the Harlequin Reader Service.
We make a portion of our mailing list available to reputable third parties that offer products we believe may interest you. If you prefer that we not exchange your name with third parties, or if you wish to clarify or modify your communication preferences, please visit us at www.ReaderService.com/consumerchoice or write to us at Harlequin Reader Service Preference Service, P.O. Box 9062, Buffalo, NY 14269. Include your complete name and address.

LIDIR13

ReaderService.com

Manage your account online!

- Review your order history
- Manage your payments
- Update your address

> ### We've designed the Harlequin® Reader Service website just for you.

Enjoy all the features!

- Reader excerpts from any series
- Respond to mailings and special monthly offers
- Discover new series available to you
- Browse the Bonus Bucks catalog
- Share your feedback

Visit us at:
ReaderService.com

All Laura White wants is a second chance.
Will she find it in Cooper Creek?

Read on for a preview of
THE COWBOY'S HEALING WAYS.

The door opened, bringing in cool air and a few stray drops of rain. The man in the doorway slipped off boots and hung a cowboy hat on a hook by the door. She watched as he shrugged out of his jacket and hung it next to his hat.

When he turned, she stared up at a man with dark hair that brushed his collar and lean, handsome features. He looked as at home in this big house as he did in his worn jeans and flannel shirt. His dark eyes studied her with curious suspicion. She'd gotten used to that look. She'd gotten used to people whispering behind their hands as she walked past.

But second chances and starting over meant wanting something new. She wanted to be the person people welcomed into their lives. She wanted to be the woman a man took a second look at, maybe a third.

Jesse Cooper took a second look, but it was a look of suspicion.

"Jesse, I'm so glad you're here." Granny Myrna had returned with a cold washcloth, which she placed on Laura's forehead. "It seems I had an accident."

"Really?" Jesse smiled a little, warming the coolness in dark eyes that focused on Laura.

"I pulled right out in front of her. She drove her car off the side of the road to keep from hitting me."

Laura closed her eyes. A cool hand touched the gash at her hairline.

"Let me see this."

She opened her eyes and he was squatting in front of her, studying the cut. He looked from the gash to her face. Then he moved and stood back up, unfolding his long legs with graceful ease. Laura clasped her hands to keep them from shaking.

A while back there had been an earthquake in Oklahoma. Laura remembered when it happened, and how they'd all wondered if they'd really felt the earth move or if it had been their imaginations. She was pretty sure it had just happened again. The earth had moved, shifting precariously as a hand touched her face and dark eyes studied her intently, with a strange mixture of curiosity, surprise and something else.

Will Jesse ever allow the mysterious Laura into his life—and his heart?

Pick up THE COWBOY'S HEALING WAYS by Brenda Minton, available in February 2013 from Love Inspired.

Love Inspired **HISTORICAL**

The wrong groom could be the
perfect match in

GROOM BY ARRANGEMENT

by **Rhonda Gibson**

Eliza Kelly thought her humiliation was complete when she
identified the wrong train passenger as her mail-order groom.
She was only trying to tell Jackson Hart that the madcap scheme
was *not* her idea. When the blacksmith decides to stay, he offers
the lovely widow a marriage of convenience. Between caring for
an orphaned youngster and protecting Eliza, Jackson feels whole
again. If only he can persuade Eliza to marry him, and fulfill
their long-buried dreams of forging a real family.

Available in February wherever books are sold.